The BULL RIDER'S KEEPER

Lynn Cahoon

Author of *The Bull Rider's Brother* and *The Bull Rider's Manager*

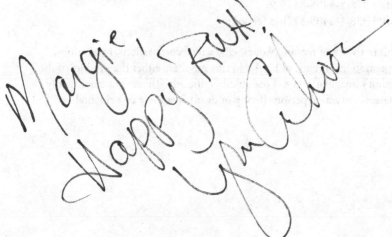

Margie,
Happy RWA!
Lynn Cahoon

Crimson Romance
New York London Toronto Sydney New Delhi

CRIMSON
ROMANCE

Crimson Romance
An Imprint of Simon & Schuster, Inc.
1230 Avenue of the Americas
New York, NY 10020

ISBN 978-1-4405-8119-9
ISBN 978-1-4405-8120-5 (ebook)

*To my own cowboy who held me up
even during the dark times.*

Acknowledgments

Big thanks to Emily Tatum, beta reader extraordinaire, as well as my CORE group. Thanks for pushing me to think past the first answer. Jess Verdi, thanks for your editing wisdom.

Jesse's story and the Bull Rider series started with my trip to a rodeo in a small town known for throwing a heck of a celebration party. My life was in upheaval at the time, but this nugget of story stayed with me. Shawnee, Idaho, might be a fictional place but the mountain valley town keeps me connected with home.

Chapter 1

Time waits for no man, and as usual, Jesse was late. Peeking in the doorway of the class that was supposed to start any minute, he breathed a sigh of relief. Professor DeMarco wasn't there. He crossed to the next door that led to her office, knocked quickly, then burst in. "Professor DeMarco, I need to leave early today ..." He stopped two steps into the room, glancing at the open door for the name plate. Right office, wrong woman. Instead of the elegant art instructor, a very curvy Venus stood in a black bra and lacy black panties, holding a privacy sheet out from her body like she didn't quite know what to do with it.

Her eyes widened as she realized he was in the room. "Get out of here!" she shrieked. Then, realizing she still held the sheet at arm's length, she grabbed it and pressed it against her body.

Jesse could have told her it was a lost cause. What he'd seen couldn't be unseen and she would be haunting his dreams for a while. Instead, he cast his glance regretfully downward and turned around. "Sorry, I guess I should have waited in the hall."

He was closing the door behind him when he heard her response.

"Neanderthal."

When she entered the classroom a few minutes later as that week's live model, he saw her gaze stop at his easel for a second. Then she did something that never happened when Jesse met a beautiful woman. She ignored him.

He glanced at his watch: ten to four. He'd promised to be at the airport no later than an hour before his plane left at six. Yet he still sat in front of his easel.

Focusing on the study he'd been working on for the entire class period, he sighed, knowing he'd missed something. The model today was exquisite, a woman who could have been not only Miss Idaho, but also Miss Freaking Universe. Her blond hair fell straight, ending in the middle of a tan, well-defined back. The girl's body showed a healthy addiction to working out.

He knew the curves that were covered by the privacy sheet, and Jesse felt his body reacting to the view. Not the most professional of reactions for an artist, especially if he wanted to be taken seriously in the art industry someday. He shifted on the stool, his attention falling on her hands. Strong hands that gripped the cloth keeping her covered. The fabric draped around her as if she'd just woken from a night of wild sex. She sat like a goddess in front of the drawing class. Long, slender fingers displayed her nails painted in that weird clear and white thing girls did. He focused on his canvas and, using his pencil, gently added a shadow to the back of the hand.

He tuned into his artist's eye, noticing the play of light off her straight hair, the gentle curve of her shoulder. Her long, regal neck. Glancing back at his sketchpad, he knew the only things he'd managed to capture from the vitality of this woman were the hands. He'd nailed the hands. A smile curved on his lips as he looked back up at the goddess in front of him to discover her staring back at him.

Heat coursed across the room, his desire hot, his feelings similar to what he often felt when he locked eyes with a gorgeous woman from across a crowded bar. But this, this felt different. His smile faded as hers gently grew. Did she know what he'd been thinking? Hell, he wanted her to know. He wanted to feel those lips against his own, uncover the body only hinted at in the crowded art room. He wanted to possess her. He felt like a teenaged boy looking at his first girlie magazine. No, this was more than youthful attraction. Their gazes locked, and he started to rise from his stool, wanting to introduce himself. To get her name, for God's sake.

A beeping from his watch broke his focus, and he dropped his gaze for a second. When he looked back, she'd turned her head away, the moment lost.

Jesse sighed and opened his case, putting away supplies. Time to go back into the real world. Time to become Jesse Sullivan, Champion Bull Rider and Professional Bull-Shitter. Eight seconds riding a bull and hours of interviews with reporters wondering why he would risk his life day after day. Wondering who Jesse Sullivan really was underneath that cowboy hat.

"Packing up already? We've got the studio for an extended period." Susan DeMarco came up behind him, staring at his drawing. "This is very good. You've captured something here, something vulnerable. I'm sure with a bit more time ..."

"Sorry, professor. I have a ride waiting for me. Start of the season, and my manager already has my weekends scheduled to the gills. I had to fight to keep these last four Fridays free so I can finish your class." Jesse stared at the image on his paper and then back at the model. He pulled himself out of the trance. "It's easy to have a quality product when you bring in models like that. She's amazing."

Susan DeMarco smiled. "I'm glad you think so. I've been meaning to introduce the two of you. That's my daughter, Taylor."

"Your daughter?" Jesse choked out, looking between mother and daughter. "Now I know I'm out of here. No matchmaking, Professor. I have plenty of buckle bunnies chasing me out there in my other life. I don't need that kind of a distraction."

He glanced around the studio at the other students, most at least five years younger and fresh out of high school. He stuck out like an old man in this group of metrosexuals, with their flip-flops and long shorts. Ever since he had started taking classes last year, he had felt out of place. Nevertheless, he kept coming back, needing to be more than the image of him painted by the reporters on the rodeo circuit.

He tapped his hand on the professor's arm in a farewell gesture as he walked past her. Susan DeMarco had been his first instructor at this school. Her gentle instruction and kind words were] part of the reason he kept coming back. No way could he be caught even thinking about what he wanted to do to her daughter. Some problems didn't need to happen. He turned on his famous bull rider smile and teased, "Besides, you know you're the one I want."

Susan laughed. "Flirting with the professor doesn't give you bonus points in my class, Mr. Sullivan, even if it has worked on other instructors."

Jesse opened the door of the classroom. "Can't blame a guy for trying. See you next week."

She followed him out into the hallway. "You're coming to the gallery opening Monday evening, right? My secretary says she hasn't received your response to the invitation."

Jesse paused, leaning against the wall. "I don't know. I do so many of those types of receptions for the job … I hate to play Jesse Sullivan on my time off."

Susan's eyes sparkled. "Then don't come as Jesse Sullivan, bull rider. Come as a serious art lover. I have no doubt you can hold your own with that group." She stepped closer. "Besides, I'd love to see you in a tux."

"Now, see, you shoot me down, then butter me back up." Jesse grinned. "As long as you don't introduce me as the bull rider-gone-artist, I'll come."

"You'll just be one of my students, I swear." Susan held her hand up in a three-fingered Girl Scout salute.

" If the airline gods smile on my travel plans, I'll be there. My plane gets in around two on Monday."

"You need me to send over a tux?" Susan glanced down at the t-shirt and Wranglers he'd worn to class. A pair of dress Tony Lamas peeked out from under the jeans. "Maybe some shoes?"

"Now don't be telling me I can't wear boots with a tux." Jesse laughed when he saw Susan flinch. "I'm kidding. It might surprise you to know I own more than just jeans and t-shirts."

"Jesse Sullivan, nothing about you would surprise me." Susan waved and re-entered the classroom.

He walked past the elevator, taking the stairs instead. When he reached the parking lot, he saw Angie's blue BMW idling near the curb. A lit cigarette hung outside the rolled-down window, and Jesse could hear the strains of Martina McBride flowing from his mother's car. Not for the first time, he wondered what life could have been like if she'd stayed home instead of running off to Vegas when he and James were kids. *If wishes were horses, all beggars would ride.*

He opened the back door, and dropped his portfolio case and supply bag on the floorboard. Angie had his overnight case and rodeo bag sitting on the seat waiting for him.

"How was school, sweetie?" His mom leaned over and kissed him on the cheek as he settled into the passenger seat.

"Kenny beat me up and stole my lunch money. Oh, wait, that happened when I was eight and you weren't there." Jesse reached back and grabbed his sponsor button-down shirt, sliding it on over the tee before he snapped his seatbelt into place. He buttoned the front and glanced at his watch. The conversation with Susan had made him later than he'd planned.

"Don't talk back to your mother." Angie checked her rearview mirror and gunned the gas, pulling the car out into traffic. "Snark isn't in your character. You're the sweet one. Your brother is the one who gives me heartache."

"Just kidding." Jesse checked his phone. Three missed calls and a terse text from Barb. The woman was an amazing manager, but just a bit anal. He texted a short reply, then looked over at Angie. "My professor tried to fix me up with her daughter."

"And when are you going out?" Angie swerved around a car that she had determined was holding them back. The airport was ten minutes away from the university in light traffic. Angie could get him there in five minutes, despite full-blown rush hour traffic. The woman had no fear.

"I said no." Jesse remembered Taylor's hands, and wondered how they would feel caressing his arms, rubbing down his back. How his hands would feel stripping her of that damn sheet. He flipped down the visor and checked his hair in the vanity mirror. He finger-combed a few stray locks, then, satisfied, flipped the visor in place. His hat would cover most of his hair anyway, at least until they were seated on the plane. Then Barb could take over the fussing.

"Heavens, why not? Is she not up to your standards?" Angie sped through the intersection as the light turned yellow.

Jesse didn't answer, only raised his eyebrows as he stared at her. He tucked in his shirt and replaced the everyday leather belt with one that had his name engraved on the back, his latest championship buckle adorning the front.

"What? It wasn't red." Angie glanced at him, her brow furrowed. "And you're trying to change the subject."

"She wasn't my type." Jesse stared out the side window. No, the woman who had sat for class today wasn't in his league. Not even close. He was a shimmer of light, and she was an exploding sun. No way would he be able to ask her out for coffee, much less anything else. What would they talk about? Professor DeMarco was out of her mind to think her daughter might say yes to a casual conversation with this bull rider who pretended to be an artist. For a moment, when their eyes had met, Jesse could see a past, present, and future with this woman all rolled up into one second. He shook his head. Maybe he'd find the one, someday. Right now, he was too busy to notice.

He watched as Angie pulled the car over to the curb and stopped in front of the airport departure area doors. After she slipped the car into park, he patted her hand. "Thanks for the ride, Mom."

"I don't know why you're keeping your classes a secret from your brother. James and Lizzie would support you." Angie shooed him away with her hand. "Just get going. And stop calling me Mom. Angie. I want you to call me Angie."

Jesse reached over the seat and grabbed his black Stetson. After he'd slipped out of the front seat and retrieved his luggage, he stuck his head back in the front door. "Love you, Mom."

He slammed the door shut and tapped on the car's roof. Putting on his hat, he watched her speed away in the little sports car. She barely missed a cab whose driver had only thought he had the right of way. As he watched Angie leave, a striking brunette climbed out of a cab that had just arrived. The girl slowed her movement when she noticed him standing there, making sure he saw enough of her to entice. Catching her eye, he put on his million-watt grin, then tipped his hat and turned away. He had business to attend to.

Jesse walked up to the curbside check-in and handed his bag to the skycap. Barb stood just inside the glass doors of the terminal, glaring at him. He lifted his hand in a wave.

"Where you headed?" the older man asked, carrying Jesse's bag to the counter.

There were so many answers to that question, but all the man really wanted to know was the next stop on Jesse's tour.

"Cody, Wyoming."

• • •

Taylor pulled on her robe, watching her mother interact with the remaining students. When she'd gotten the call this morning, she had wondered if maybe things were finally getting better between them. Stupid. Mom never just wanted to see her. No, it was always about something someone needed. And she continued to act like the dutiful daughter. Old habits die hard. She grabbed her bag and hurried into the bathroom attached to her mom's office. Despite her working at a state university, Susan DeMarco got the best of everything. Of course, it didn't hurt that her family owned the oldest art gallery in Boise, and they donated heavily toward the university's public art program.

"It's part of the image," her mother would chirp if Taylor ever questioned their funding of some off-the-wall projects. At least she'd only had to work for the western art exhibit last year. Finding unknown and upcoming artists was like mining for diamonds or panning for gold. She smiled at the analogy.

Main Street Gallery was thriving under her control. They'd had some tough times in the past, but she knew if she could just get through December, she'd have her first year in the black. They had a major show next Monday, and she should have been at the gallery finalizing details instead of sitting for her mom's class.

She thought about the man in the last row. He'd left early, right after she had caught him staring at her. Of course, that was what they were supposed to do—watch and draw—but for some reason, his attention had felt different. Like he could read her mind, or something. She shivered. Too bad she didn't have time for a quick relationship. She had to get the gallery's profit margin up soon. Her parents had dropped too many hints that they were running out of patience with her management. Taylor found herself remembering how the man had focused on the canvas. Then he'd turned those artist eyes on her, poring over her body so deeply that, sometimes, she had thought he could see through the drape. Hell, he'd seen her practically naked before class started— he had probably kept replaying the tape in his head of barging in on her. When the other men, little more than boys, in class looked at her, she felt naked, exposed. However, when that tall hunk of muscular man in the back stared, she'd felt a different emotion flow from him. She'd felt reverence. She blew out an exasperated sigh. Typical, she was reading too much into a look. Assuming the best out of men always caused her trouble.

She was losing perspective. Ever since Brad had dumped her with the old, "it's not you, it's me" line, she'd been gun shy. Especially, since she'd found out he had been seeing other women while she was in the middle of planning their wedding.

There couldn't have been that strong of a connection with the hot guy in the class; they hadn't said a word to each other. However, for one second, when their gazes had locked, she'd felt drawn to him. It was the same feeling she got when she fell in love with a painting and, later, the artist. She was unable to tear her eyes away.

She pulled on her designer jeans and silky peach shirt. Slipping into her bejeweled flip-flops, she checked her messages. She texted a few responses to Brit back at the gallery. Brit had been her best friend in high school and now was more than an assistant. She swore the girl could read her mind. Hours spent together developing new shows and finding new artists had a tendency to do that to people.

Her stomach growled, and she glanced at the office door. She just had to wait for her mother to stop holding court with her students so Taylor could get out of there. Looking out the large window, she watched the river winding past the campus. A few joggers were running the greenbelt. The shop had kept her too busy. She hadn't been running in weeks; her body yearned for the release.

Working downtown, Taylor never came to this part of Boise unless she was visiting or dropping off work from the gallery. Next year, if the gallery made it to the black and she had enough saved for a down payment on a house, she would consider buying in the nearby neighborhood. She'd need to see if she could find something far enough away to avoid the frat parties but close enough to walk to the campus for events. Or, maybe she'd buy a condo downtown overlooking the river. One good year with the gallery and she'd have her place.

Her thoughts were still lost in possible real estate choices when she felt her mom's touch on her arm.

"Thanks for coming today. I don't know what I would have done if you couldn't have gotten away." Her mom walked behind the old oak desk and slipped off her high heels, replacing them with a pair of ballerina flats. "I promised them a live model. How many times can you draw a bowl of fruit?"

Taylor turned away from the window. "As good as you look, you could have modeled for the class."

Her mother laughed the tinkling laugh Taylor loved. "First Jesse Sullivan flirts with me, and now you're being sweet? What happened? Is the moon blue?"

"Face it, Mom, you're still hot." Taylor grabbed her Vera bag, slipping it over her shoulder. "I've got to get back to the gallery."

Her mom's phone beeped with a text. *Here we go*, Taylor thought. The dean probably needed her to chair some black-tie charity event. Her mom read the message, then quickly keyed in a response, her fingers flying on the touch screen. Finished, she slipped the phone into her purse, and put her arm around Taylor.

"Come, have lunch with us. Your dad is waiting at that little Mexican place you love." Susan paused at the door to lock the office, jangling her keys. "You drive. He'll take me home after we eat."

Taylor inwardly groaned. She'd assumed modeling for her mom's art class had been the favor of the day. If they were having lunch with her father, well, that meant the world was ending. He never took time out of his day for family matters. *Please, don't let it be the gallery*, she thought, throwing the wish into the universe.

As she followed her mom, she couldn't squelch the bad feeling growing in her stomach.

No matter where Taylor parked, her car always drew a crowd. Today, several guys hung around it, checking out the interior and rims, and challenging each other on the engine size. When she climbed into the driver's side, she heard one of the young men tell the group, "I bet she has a sugar daddy."

"Keep guessing," she called back as she shoved the stick into reverse and backed out of the parking spot. She revved the motor and sped out onto the road, heading to the turnoff where the family-owned restaurant sat tucked into a side street, bordered by a residential area. Maria's had been in business long before the current planning and zoning laws that frowned on the mixed-use concept came into existence. Her mom turned from staring out the open window to look at her daughter. "How are the preparations coming for Monday's show? Is John excited?"

Now Taylor knew something had to be wrong. No way would her mom miss an opportunity to correct her on even the slightest error in good manners. "The guy is over the moon. He's been in the gallery this week more than I have. He keeps changing his mind about the placement of the paintings. Today, I had to give him a deadline and told Brit to kick him out at noon."

"Tortured artists are a handful." Her mom smiled, her gaze distant. "I remember my first show when your grandfather ran the gallery. He made all the placement decisions. I knew I was going to fall flat and not sell a single item."

Taylor pulled the sports car into a slot in front of the restaurant. She looked at her mom as she turned off the car, hoping her face would give away a clue to the real purpose of this impromptu family meeting. "And yet, you sold out."

All she got was her mom's bright smile in response. "Which caused your grandfather to send me on a trip to Paris to study at the Musée du Louvre. Your grandfather didn't want me to be successful too quickly." She dropped her voice in an imitation of the man. "Fast success creates lazy work."

Susan laughed, then slipped out of the car and headed into the restaurant. She appeared to be in a hurry, or didn't want to be alone with Taylor any longer than the short drive. Taylor scurried after her mom into Maria's.

The smell of grilled onions and peppers hit her as soon as she opened the yellow door, causing her mouth to water. She smiled at the hostess who was dressed in a white peasant blouse and a colored, tiered skirt. The satin shimmered as the girl walked them to the booth where Taylor's dad was seated. The lunch crowd had thinned. They were the only customers except for a young couple seated near the door.

Her dad stood to let her mom slide into the upholstered booth. Married thirty years, and he still treated her mother like a princess, delicate to the touch. His blue eyes sparkled as he watched his wife settle, then he turned his gaze on Taylor. He was still striking at his age, with salt and pepper hair, and laugh lines etched near his eyes. After all these years, her parents were still deeply in love.

"Hi, Dad." She reached up on her tiptoes to kiss his cheek. "What brings you out with family on a weekday? No one else to schmooze?"

He put his hands on her arms and pulled her into a hug. When he released her, he pointed to the other bench. "Have a seat. Your mother and I want to talk to you."

Taylor widened her eyes and tried for a shocked expression. "I can't believe it. I thought my parents just wanted to have lunch with me. If this is about me moving out, you know I'm starting to look at places. I just want to make sure I don't buy in haste and then regret the purchase. It's a big step."

Her father waved away the notion with a large, gnarled hand. He'd worked as a mechanic when he had met her mom, and he still loved tinkering with the old classics in the garage. Her mom hated his hobby, but he'd restored Taylor's MGB for her high school graduation gift. "You can stay in the house as long as you need. We barely see you, anyway."

"Then why the clandestine lunch meeting?" Taylor leaned back as the waitress delivered her shrimp fajitas and her mom's three-cheese taco salad. Her dad had ordered for them. She would normally argue about that, but they both knew she would have ordered the same thing. She pulled out a warmed tortilla and started to layer the veggies, toppings, and shrimp on top.

"We just wanted to touch base with you." His gaze darted back to her mom. "How are things at the gallery?"

Not the question she expected. "Besides being crazy busy getting ready for Monday's opening? Fine, I guess. Brit's been a lifesaver during the last month. I swear that girl could sell a toddler's crayon drawing." Taylor laughed. "You'll never believe it, but she sold the last of the Markus prints to a collector last week."

"The guy who was just arrested for trying to hold up a liquor store in his underwear last month?" Her dad laughed. "I thought we'd be stuck with his inventory for years."

"Apparently, Brit convinced the guy that, since the artist would be unavailable for additional work for the next five-to-ten, his current pieces would be worth money down the line." Taylor took a sip of water. "I swear, she's Molly Sunshine, sometimes."

"Brit's a good employee." Her mother focused on her salad, not looking up as she added, "Have you considered going to Europe this summer? You work so hard, maybe you need a break."

Taylor shook her head. "No way can I get away for more than a weekend this year. We've got some amazing shows lined up in the next few months. With the longer days, and the city's promotion trying to get people downtown on Wednesdays, we'll be busier than ever."

She watched her parents exchange a look and thought she saw her mother's head shake in a silent message not to say anything. They were keeping something from her, she could tell.

"Are you seeing anyone?" The question came out of nowhere.

Taylor smiled, catching on to their little secret. They were trying to set her up for a blind date, probably with one of her father's many associates. An up-and-coming success story who was just perfect for her, since they were both single.

"Really, guys, I'm too involved with the gallery right now to even consider casual dating. If you're concerned I'm still hung up on Brad, believe me, that's not an issue. I just haven't found Mr. Right." Taylor's thoughts went to the man from class. "Someday, I promise, you'll have grandchildren. Just not tomorrow."

"We just worry about you." Her dad checked his watch. "I didn't realize it was already this late." He turned to her mother. "Ready, dear?"

Her mother pushed aside her half-eaten lunch. "I have some calls to make for the club that I've been putting off." She stood and kissed Taylor on the cheek as her father threw some bills on the table. "We'll see you later?"

"I'm planning on spending the weekend at the gallery, so don't expect to see me much before Monday night." Taylor watched her parents glance at each other again and groaned. They were matchmaking. Monday night there would be an extra man at the opening, who just so happened to stop in. "Look, I'm fine. Busy, but fine."

Her father patted her hand. "We know you are. Just remember that we love you."

Without another word, her parents hurried out of the restaurant, their heads together, whispering. Taylor watched them leave, knowing she was doomed to play nice with some guy on Monday. She didn't have time for their games.

The waitress came by to clear off their plates. "Can I get you something else?"

Taylor glanced at her lunch. Might as well eat now; she'd probably be working late tonight. "Bring me a frozen margarita."

After spending quality time with her folks, she needed a drink.

Chapter 2

Taylor pulled up the top of her gold sequined dress once more as she looked in the mirror. She should have gone with her instincts and worn the blue halter. In this strapless outfit, she'd be constantly checking to make sure that the top wasn't showing too much skin. She had to look like a professional. She looked at herself in the mirror, and the face of Main Street Gallery looked back at her. She'd studied for years at every art institution in the Northwest, trying to learn as much as she needed to be as good a manager as her grandfather had been. The place was her birthright, her heritage. No way would she let the Harrison name down. She sat on the edge of her bed, reaching out to scratch Miss Fitz's stomach. The cocker was older than Taylor wanted to admit, but seemed to be in good health.

"Who's a good dog?" She leaned in and gave Miss Fitz a kiss on the top of her buff-colored head. The dog wagged her tail and looked up expectantly.

"No walk tonight, buddy." She pulled at the bodice one more time to make sure it was holding fast, and then grabbed her purse and keys. She had fifteen minutes to get across town so she could be in the gallery before the doors opened. She needed to double-check the details for the party. Time to show her parents that she was a confident and successful executive. Being late wouldn't make the right impression.

She pressed a kiss to her grandfather's picture on her dresser mirror and sprayed perfume on her neck as the finishing touch.

•••

An hour later, the party was in full swing. Showcasing a new artist always worried her; she never knew if people would be interested enough in the promotion to take time out to attend an opening. Luckily, most of the art-buying players in Boise had returned to attending shows and opening their wallets a tad. The recession had hit the town pretty hard, but if the level of art purchases were any indication, they were starting to see an upturn. John was one of Taylor's discoveries. She'd found him at a flea market, selling paintings for cheap to cover his rent. Taylor had given him her business card. Within a week, she'd contracted his collections. He had an amazing eye for a landscape artist, and many of the pieces they were showing tonight were of local spots Taylor knew people would recognize.

"You won't believe this." Brit handed her a glass of champagne. Taylor's assistant wore a long black halter dress with a plunging neckline. It accented her figure, yet she still looked elegant. The girl could pull off a gunnysack.

"Don't tell me something's wrong. The caterers are out of food. The wine's gone?" Taylor's eyes widened. "The bathroom backed up."

Brit slapped her on the arm. "You're such a Negative Nancy. Why does something have to be wrong?"

Taylor breathed in a sigh of relief. "Things just seem to happen that way. You had me going for a minute. So what's up?"

Brit took a sip from her glass. "The toilets are overflowing."

Taylor choked. "What?"

Brit patted her on the back as Taylor coughed up champagne that had gone down the wrong tube. Taylor's eyes watered. "Lighten up, I was kidding. But glad to know what gets you all freaked."

"You're not right, you know that?" Taylor dabbed at her eyes with a napkin, hoping her tears hadn't wrecked her eye makeup.

"Don't hate." Brit raised her eyebrows. "Besides, I bring good news. We've already sold five of John's paintings tonight."

"Shut up." Taylor wanted to squeal, or jump up and down, but her stilettos didn't seem sturdy enough. "You're teasing."

"On my honor, I swear." Brit grinned. "John's over the moon. He's been telling everyone how wonderful you are because you believed in him. I think he sang 'Wind Beneath My Wings' a few times."

"I'm so happy for him. I should go congratulate him." Taylor searched the crowd, her gaze landing on her parents. They were talking to that hunk who had been in her mom's drawing class. Wow, did the boy clean up good. She dropped her gaze down the length of his body, her breath catching a bit. If she weren't on the clock tonight, he'd be in big trouble. It wouldn't hurt her to be social for a few minutes. In fact, it would be rude not to say hello. She strolled toward the trio.

"Where are you going? John is on the other side of the gallery," Brit called after her.

"Just checking in with the folks. Tell John I'll be right there." Taylor weaved her way through the crowd, grabbed a fresh glass from a waiter, and slid in next to her father. The three stopped talking and looked at her.

"Hey, pumpkin." Her father beamed down at her. "You look great when you put on a dress. Need to do that more often."

"Stop messing with her. Jesse Sullivan, you remember my daughter, Taylor?" Her mom lightly pushed Jesse closer.

The hunk, now known as Jesse, leaned forward and tapped his forehead in some sort of salute. "Good evening, Miss DeMarco."

"Taylor, please." Taylor tugged at the arm of her father's jacket. "You'll never believe this, but John's already sold five pieces."

"See, Jesse, I told you that you won't regret this decision. John is just one of the many talented new artists my daughter has signed with the gallery." Her father gave her a little squeeze.

Taylor tilted her head. "Oh, did you buy one of the paintings?" The man hadn't looked like anything more than a student when she saw him in class. Of course, that didn't mean he hadn't come from money.

Jesse smiled. "You could say that."

Her dad slapped him on the back. "Honey, you're looking at the new owner of Main Street Gallery. Jesse just bought me out."

• • •

Jesse watched the surprise fill Taylor's face, then another emotion—anger? He must be misreading her. He'd just committed way too much of his personal winnings in an art gallery. Barb would kill him when she found out. He'd throw in a promise to ride for at least a few more seasons, just to make sure he didn't lose everything. He should have waited. He should have said he'd think about it. However, when Professor DeMarco's husband had mentioned that they were putting the gallery on the market, the words just fell out of his mouth.

It was typical Jesse Sullivan style. Talk first, ask questions later. Man, the family was going to laugh their asses off when he told them. The good news was that Mr. DeMarco had promised Taylor would stay on and manage the place, for the right salary. Jesse's stomach rolled. He owned a business. He was the man. How could he be the man? He didn't know anything about corporations, or businesses, or, his conscience added, art.

"I'm looking forward to working with you," he said. Whatever he'd expected, it hadn't been this silent treatment. "I'm meeting with your father and my people tomorrow at the gallery. Do you want to join us?"

Her eyes widened and Jesse wondered if he'd said something wrong. Finally, she took a deep breath.

"I've got to go congratulate our artist." She glanced at her dad and mom, who watched her very carefully. "Someone has to work around here."

She spun around and Jesse watched her full skirt twirl. His fingers ached to pick up a pencil and start drawing the folds of that dress. Man, this girl got to him in ways he'd never imagined. Now he had to work with her on a daily basis. He was good and totally screwed.

Mr. DeMarco stared at the retreating form of his daughter. Finally, Susan broke the uncomfortable silence. "Rich, why don't you take Jesse around the gallery and show him what he's gotten himself into. Maybe we need to let him think on his decision for a while."

Yes, Jesse's mind screamed, *an escape hatch*. He watched Taylor across the room, her hand on the artist's arm as she threw her head back to laugh. He felt a stab of jealousy as she smiled at something the man said. Back out, now. Leave, and never return. Don't throw good money after bad. Run. He thought all these things, and more. When he opened his mouth to speak, he said something that surprised him.

"I don't want to back out. I want to buy the gallery, if you'll sell it to me." Jesse broke his gaze from watching Taylor and turned it back on the couple in front of him.

Rich slapped him on the back. "Now that's what I like. A man who knows his mind."

As they walked through the building Jesse had just bought, he thought about Rich's pronouncement. The one thing Jesse had never been was someone who knew his own mind.

What in the world had he done?

• • •

The next morning he pulled the gang together for a family meeting. His family asked him that very same question more than once. His brother James and his brother's wife Lizzie had Skyped into the meeting from their home in the mountains. Jesse could see their worried faces fill the laptop's screen. Barb paced the kitchen where he and Angie sat around the computer.

"Maybe we should let Jesse talk," his mother said again. Everyone had been talking over each other since he'd announced his plans to buy Main Street Gallery. No one listened, and the voices grew louder.

Jesse saw Angie grab her purse, and wondered if his mother had had enough and was planning a getaway. The woman didn't deal with conflict, that he knew. An ear splitting horn pierced the cacophony of voices and the kitchen fell silent. Angie held an air horn in her hand. As she glanced around the room, she said, "Why don't we let Jesse talk now?"

Barb stopped pacing and sat down at the table across from Jesse, glaring at Angie. "Like I can hear anything now, anyway."

"You should have listened earlier." Angie shrugged. Jesse tried not to smile. His mother had her own way of dealing with issues. Years in Las Vegas, married to what Jesse assumed was a low-level mob boss, had hardened the woman just a tad. Now she was trying to make amends to her family. Jesse gave her props for trying.

Jesse felt the attention slip from Angie to him. Nervous, he took a sip of coffee from the cup in front of him and almost choked. He glanced at his mother; she'd poured a shot of whiskey in the cup before she'd brought it to him. He blessed her for the liquid courage.

"I bought Main Street Gallery last night," Jesse said. This had been as far as he'd gotten the first time before the room had erupted in chaos. He swallowed and went on. "I think it will be a good investment. And I have the money set aside, so I don't know why you're all so upset."

Barb looked at him. "Jesse, you know that the initial investment isn't all the money this is going to cost you. Have you looked at the company's financials? Is it even making the rent? Alternatively, is payroll covered? People don't sell profitable businesses, and in this economy, art isn't high on most people's lists of must-buys."

"No, food is more important." James spoke next. "Face it, Jesse, you got bamboozled. They were looking for a sucker, and you walked into their trap." He glanced at Lizzie who had picked up one of the twins waving at the computer, trying to get Angie's attention. "How'd they even find you? Or was this done over a few drinks?"

"The gallery has a great reputation. It's one of the oldest, privately owned galleries in town. Artists who get their stuff in a show there take off; they've launched a lot of new talent." Jesse said.

"And how would you know that?" James asked. "I'm sure a history of a local galleries wasn't included in your finance classes at school."

Angie nodded, encouraging him.

He took a breath. *In for a penny ...* "I'm not majoring in finance. I've been taking art classes."

The room stayed quiet. No one spoke until, finally, Angie piped up. "And he's good, damn good."

James shook his head. "I don't believe you know what you've gotten yourself into, bro. Nevertheless, one thing's for sure: it's your money. Just don't expect the rest of us to bail you out if you get in a jam."

"Look, I'm not asking for money. Hell, I'm not even quitting riding." When she heard Jesse's words, Barb's shoulders dropped in relief. "In fact, I'm probably going to have to ride at least another year. I'd planned on going out on top this year, but I'd like to build my savings back up before I charge into this full time."

"I think you're too late for that," James said. Lizzie elbowed him, and he shot her a look. He leaned back and sighed. "But if this is what you want, we'll support you."

"Thanks." Jesse glanced at Barb. As his manager, she could make his life hell for the next two years. "So, you on the Jesse train?"

Barb leaned back too, resigned to the idea. "I can't say I like it. I don't think a man can serve two masters. You know bull riding at your level isn't just about the weekends. You'll need a strong manager at the gallery to handle things when you're not available. You got anyone you can trust?"

"I've already thought of that. The current manager, Taylor. Her folks said she'd probably stay on, if I made it worth her time."

"I knew there was a girl in this somewhere," James said.

Jesse shook his head. "Believe me, she's not interested in me. I don't think she dates cowboys. More of a suit kind of gal."

Angie laughed. "Son, you don't get it, do you."

Jesse focused in on his mother. "What?"

"Every woman wants a cowboy. And now that you've bought the gallery, she knows you're not some ranch hand." Angie smiled and waved at the little boy on the computer screen, who giggled and waved even harder in response. She returned her gaze to Jesse. "You're now irresistible."

Jesse thought about the look Taylor had given him when her folks told her that he was her new boss. Hate, loathing, pain. Many emotions had floated through that look, but admiration or lust weren't even in the ballpark. "I think you're wrong, Mom. The woman hates me." Of course, he'd probably messed up any chance of a relationship—professional or otherwise—when he walked in on her getting ready to model for the class. Seeing a woman naked tended to stick with a guy.

"Even more reason to get rid of her and put your own manager into the gallery." Barb glanced at Angie. "Jesse's going to be out of town the next three weekends. You want to play gallery owner for him?"

Angie tapped her purple-starred nails on the table. She glanced at Jesse, then back at Barb. "You know, I've been thinking I need something to do with my time. I'd love to."

Jesse nodded. "I think it's smart. I mean, I don't want to get rid of Taylor unless I have to, but at least with Mom there, I'd have some sort of connection to the place while I'm out of town. Look, I know I'm asking for your support after the fact."

James muttered, "Typical Jesse."

His brother's words brought heat to Jesse's face. "I'm the family screw-up, I get that. But I'd really appreciate your support with this. We've always been there for each other. I'd like to think you back me on this decision." He glanced at the clock. "I was supposed to meet the DeMarcos at the gallery today."

Barb shook her head. "We need to slow this down a little. Give you some time to think out your options. I'll call and set something up for tomorrow. So the family is supporting this?" Barb glanced around the room, focusing on each person to get consent before she continued. James took the longest to meet her eyes but even he finally nodded. "Then it's settled. I'll go over, introduce Angie and myself, and get an accountant set up to go over the books. I'm assuming George will be handling the legal stuff?"

Jesse nodded. George Baxter had been his and James's lawyer for years. "Would you call him and have him contact the DeMarcos to start pulling together a contract?"

"I'll talk to him this afternoon. Angie? Can you meet me there tomorrow?" Barb glanced at Angie's nails and added, "Unless you're busy."

"Honey, nothing is more important than when my boy needs me." Angie focused her attention on Lizzie and James. "Sorry, loves, I won't be up there this weekend. Expect me bright and early next Monday though. Grandma Angie needs her grandkid fix."

Jesse heard JR, his nephew, laugh in the background.

He made his goodbyes to his brother and sister-in-law and promised to come up to Shawnee to visit as soon as possible. Angie and Barb were discussing their plans for meeting up the next morning. He caught his mother's attention. "So how come Grandma Angie's fine, but I can't call you Mom?"

Angie shrugged. "The babies don't know better. They love me. I just don't want some great catch hearing you call me Mom and thinking I'm old, or something."

Barb pursed her lips together and Jesse knew she was holding in a laugh. "So tell me about this Taylor. Is she going to give us trouble?"

Jesse thought about the woman who'd posed half nude so effortlessly for a group of college students. He remembered the way she floated through the gallery patrons Monday night, smiling and joking, even after her parents had announced the sale. She had steel balls, that one. He realized the women were waiting for an answer. An answer he wasn't sure about. Finally, he said the only thing that he knew to be true. "I don't know."

Barb cocked her head and watched him. "Usually, you can size someone up in a few minutes and know if they are going to be trouble or not. What's different about this girl? Or, have you not met her yet?"

Jesse took another swig of the laced coffee before he answered. "I've met her, and I still don't know. She's strong, and amazing, and beautiful, but I think she's hiding something inside, really, really deep." He shook his head. "Sorry, I can't answer your question."

"You like her." Barb didn't phrase it as a question, just a matter of fact.

He shook his head, and drained the coffee. "I don't know her well enough to like or hate her. All I know is, she didn't look happy to hear the news."

Barb's cell went off. She held up a finger walking away from the table as she answered, "Hi, Kadi." Barb had married into a ready-made family last year, complete with a seven—now eight—year-old who loved to ride almost as much as Jesse did. The kid had a strong seat as she rode, and she'd started competing already. Soon Kadi would be barrel racing, and Barb would have to hire someone to manage the kid's career, or give up the bull riders.

Angie stood and took Jesse's cup to the counter.

"Just coffee, please. I don't need to be drunk at ten in the morning," Jesse called after her.

Angie cocked her head. "I don't know what you're talking about."

When Angie and the coffee returned, Jesse took a tentative sip and smiled. Strong, hot, deep coffee, and only coffee. "Thanks, Mom."

She patted his shoulder. "Anytime."

Barb finished her conversation, and came over to the table. "I've got to go. Kadi forgot her riding gear, and her instructor is picking her up after school to practice for the competition this weekend."

"I'll meet you over at the gallery tomorrow." Angie smiled. "It will be like I've got a real job."

Barb and Jesse laughed.

"What?" Angie looked from one to the other.

"They won't know what hit them." Jesse patted her hand.

Barb said, "Just meet me there. We'll talk about what you need to do when we meet with this Taylor girl. Remember, you're there to protect Jesse's interest, not make friends." Barb swung her bag over her shoulder. "I'll call tonight after I talk to George."

"Thanks, Barb," Jesse called after her. She raised a hand and waved, but didn't look back as she walked to the door.

"That girl needs to put her foot down. The kid runs both Barb and Hunter with a crook of her finger." Angie shook her head.

"Mom, I'm not sure parenting advice is your forte." Jesse pulled the computer closer and opened up the website for the gallery. He sighed as they paged through the site. Finally, he leaned back and looked at his mother. "Do you think I made a mistake?"

"Heavens, no. Sometimes, fate takes an active hand in our lives. Something drew you to make that decision last night. It may have been rash, but I believe that you need to be there." She pulled out her phone. "I can get you an appointment with Angelic if you want."

"I don't need to go to a fortune teller." Jesse glanced at his watch. "But I do need to get to class." He stood and kissed his mother on the head. "You want to have dinner tonight?"

Angie nodded. "I'll visit Angelic myself. Sometimes she can feel the energy of you boys just by reading me. She's very powerful."

She's very convincing, Jesse thought. But if it made his mother happy, what was the harm.

Two hours later, he'd finished class and was heading to the gym for a quick workout when he got the answer to that question. His mom's number came up on his phone.

"Hey, Mom, I'm heading into the gym."

"You can't buy the gallery." Her voice sounded choppy and breathless.

"Hold on, what's wrong?" Jesse pulled the car into the gym's parking lot and turned off the engine.

"You can't buy the gallery. Angelic says it's a bad time for change."

Jesse smiled as he grabbed his workout bag. "Mom, you know I don't believe in psychics."

"But, Jesse, she already knew when I walked in. She was so upset. She said the same thing Barb said."

"What's that?" Jesse watched a tan, fit woman leave the gym. He'd gotten his share of dates from this place. Who needed bars anymore?

"A man can't serve two masters. He will be forced to choose."

"Look, I'm here. Can we talk about this tonight?" Jesse pulled his keys from the ignition and waited for the answer.

"She drew the death card, Jesse. If you buy the gallery, someone's going to die."

Chapter 3

Taylor sat at her desk and acted like she was going over the sale records for Monday's show. Instead, she kept playing the recurring image in her head of her dad showing Jesse Sullivan around the gallery like the papers had already been signed. After the gallery closed, she'd tried to talk to her parents, tried to get them to change their minds. Like always, they refused to listen. Her father had even patted her on the head and told her to be a good girl.

They usually discounted her feelings. When she'd wanted to take riding lessons instead of ballet, she'd been denied. Then, when she'd wanted to try out for the cheerleading squad, her mom had said no, offering instead a private gymnastics tutor. She hadn't even been able to choose her own college. Instead, she had attended Albertsons, because it was expected of a Harrison to attend the college her great grandfather had funded in its infancy. No wonder she'd fallen for Brad so quickly; the man had let her do whatever she'd wanted. Mostly, she now knew, so he'd have more time for his own extracurricular activities.

Well, she would show them good girl. This wasn't a teenage wish; this was her life they were messing with. She pulled out her planner and flipped through the address book until she found the number she was looking for. Then she dialed.

"Hawley Law Offices," said a bored receptionist.

"Michael Hawley, please." Taylor waited to be transferred and mulled the idea over in her head. This was extreme, but she had to try. For the sake of the gallery, and her own sanity, she had to try.

"Michael Hawley, speaking." A male voice interrupted her thoughts.

"Mike, it's Taylor DeMarco. I need a lawyer." She told him what she wanted to do, how she needed to find a way to save her gallery.

"It's a long shot, Taylor. I mean, your folks are both pretty high up on the power food chain. We may not even get a judge to grant us a hearing, let alone a stay of sale."

"But you'll try?" Taylor pleaded. The silence on the phone made her cringe as she waited for an answer. Then she heard his sigh.

"Yes, I'll try. We're both probably committing professional suicide here. You know that, right?"

"All I know is that I have to do everything in my power to keep control of the gallery in my family. My grandfather would roll over in his grave if he knew it was being sold."

"You're going to owe me big on this one, Taylor." Mike said his goodbyes and ended the conversation.

Taylor updated her online calendar and added the meeting with Mike. While she was checking her e-mail for incoming orders, Brit came into the office and poured herself a cup of coffee. Her assistant lounged in one of the chairs in front of Taylor's desk, her leg draped over the arm of the chair. Taylor raised an eyebrow, taking in Brit's skinny jeans and knee-high leather boots. The girl's dark hair was pulled back into a stark ponytail.

"Good morning. Auditioning for a Robert Palmer video today?" Taylor said.

"Don't be mean. John's after-closing party kept me up late. Man, he knows some wild people. You so should have come with us. We took over the top of the Hoff building after-hours. It was wicked." Brit sipped her coffee.

"I had some business to deal with …" Taylor said. "I've got a meeting out of the office this afternoon, can you handle things?"

Brit eyed her. "Can't be a nail appointment, you just got them done for the opening. Maybe a new cut? Or, are you finally going to try out that new masseuse over at Warm Springs Spa? I hear he's hot."

"Maybe I didn't tell you where my appointment was because I didn't want you to know?" Taylor smiled at her friend. Brit had joined the gallery the same summer Taylor had come to work for her grandfather. Taylor had expected to have years to learn the industry under his guidance. Instead, when he'd died last year from a stroke, she'd stepped up and started managing the gallery. And other than dealing with the mess the recession had put them in, she thought she'd been doing a pretty good job. Until last night.

"Speaking of hot guys, who was that hunk of hot with your folks last night? Everyone at the party was buzzing about him. No one knew him, so we called him your mystery date." Brit leaned forward. "I mean, did you see his eyes? I've never seen that shade of blue before. And the way his tuxedo fit ... Dude, I wanted to show him our back room, if you know what I mean."

Taylor smiled. She knew exactly what Brit meant. Jesse Sullivan had turned many heads last night, and not just those of the young women. Some of the country club members had wandered over with their cocktails to meet the mysterious man. They had used their free hands to caress his muscular arms hiding under the fabric of his jacket. The man drew women in like flies. How could she compete with that? Gallery groupies would buy stock just to spend time with the new owner. She cringed as she realized how likely that was.

"Over my dead body," she said to herself. This was her legacy. She wasn't giving in that easy.

Brit's eyes widened and Taylor realized she had said the words aloud.

Her assistant held up her hands in mock surrender. "All you had to say was that he's yours. You know I don't play in other people's backyards."

Taylor shook her head. "Sorry, I ..." She paused. How much did she want to tell Brit? And how long did she have before the news came out, anyway? "Look, things are complicated right now."

Brit picked up the sales paperwork that Taylor had already processed, and cradled the stack in her arms. Watching Taylor, she frowned. "I'm not judging or being nosy, but if you want to talk, you know I'm here. You look like someone ran over your dog and stole your truck."

"In other words, I look like a real life country song?"

"Exactly." Brit stopped at the doorway to the office. "You want me to order lunch?"

The thought of food made Taylor's stomach lurch. "No, I'll grab something while I'm out."

Her office fell silent once Brit left. Taylor stared at a framed picture on her desk. It showed the day of her first gallery opening. William Harrison had his arm around her, and a smile the size of a Golden-Day Hollywood star. She had to fix this, one way or another.

• • •

Jesse sat waiting at a plastic table under a multicolored umbrella with a big beer logo painted on it. He'd agreed to meet Angie for dinner at the downtown restaurant to try to calm her down. The woman loved her psychics.

He was nursing a longneck when he saw her, the girl he couldn't get off his mind. He'd been wrong about her hair color. What had looked like blond in the artificial light of the studio and the gallery shimmered with a touch of strawberry in the sunlight. His mouth twitched. The woman got to him. He watched her stride down the sidewalk. She was leaving one of the office buildings that mixed in with the retail and food shops lining Main Street; he knew he needed to stay away. The woman screamed danger.

Danger he'd love to unwrap. One piece of clothing at a time.

A man dashed out of the doorway she'd just vacated and jogged to catch up with her. He must have called her name, because Taylor turned and stopped, letting the man catch up. The two talked for a minute; then, he put his arm around her and they walked down the sidewalk together. It never failed—Jesse could fall faster for an unavailable, off-the-market woman than anyone in history. And he never poached.

Still, something kept him watching. Hoping for a sign that what he saw wasn't what he thought it was. A small part of him hoped she would stomp on his foot or slap the man across the face. Then Jesse could run over and save her from the leech.

"Who are you staring at?" Angie's voice broke his concentration. He stood, greeting her with a kiss on the cheek.

"Just people watching." Jesse didn't know why he lied. For some reason it felt like his mom had intruded on something extremely personal. He nodded to the bucket full of bottles on ice he'd ordered earlier. "Beer?"

Angie glanced back up the street to where Taylor and the Leech were walking into a different café with sidewalk seating. They sat down, obviously having dinner. Jesse realized Angie was no longer looking across the street, but was staring directly at him.

"Someone you know?" She nodded toward the other café.

Jesse sighed, pulling a bottle out of the bucket. He wiped off the moisture, twisted off the top, and handed it to his mother. "The woman who just sat down over there?"

"The one in the Michael Kors outfit?" Angie squinted. "Or, it could be a knock off, I can't really tell from here."

"The one in the blue, she's sitting with the man in the suit." Jesse pointed, hoping she wouldn't notice them staring. That'd be hard to explain.

"So, who is she?" Angie took a swig from her beer bottle. "I love ice-cold beer on a hot day like today."

"Good to know." Jesse wondered if Angie could handle helping out at the gallery. Her thought process wasn't quite linear. "She is my new gallery manager."

"You mean, the one I'm meeting tomorrow?" Angie squinted, sighed, and pulled her purse to her lap. She dug around for a few seconds, coming up with a pair of red prescription glasses. She slipped them on and looked at Jesse, who stared at her like she'd grown a second head. "What? A girl has to have some secrets. My eye doctor says I have the vision of a twenty-year-old; these just help my farsightedness."

Long seconds passed as Jesse watched his mom stare across the street at his new employee. Finally, Angie slipped off her glasses and put them back in their case, returning it to her purse. "She's pretty."

Freaking beautiful, Jesse thought. He just nodded. "And from what I can tell, smart."

"You're taken with her, Jesse Sullivan." She shook her finger at him when he started to rebut her statement. "A mother always knows. I knew it the first time I saw James and Lizzie look at each other. Love, it's hard to hide."

"James and Lizzie were always that way. Even back in high school, I used to rib him about being her puppy dog. But the guy had it bad. I shouldn't have made him come on tour with me."

Angie laid her hand on his forearm. "No use crying over spilled sangria. Things happen in life. You didn't make your brother do anything."

"So why does it feel like I did?" Jesse said, more to himself than his mother. "No worries, I'm not racked with guilt. I'm just thinking about some of my past decisions." *And future ones*, he added silently.

"My sweet boy." She patted his arm. Finishing off her beer, she grabbed a second one before she set down the first bottle.

Jesse waved a waitress over and took the full bottle away from his mom, setting it back in the bucket. "After we get some food."

Jesse ordered his dinner, added a few items to Angie's order, and asked the waitress to bring them a couple of iced teas as well.

The two sat without talking for a few minutes after the waitress left.

"I can't believe I bought a gallery." Jesse finally broke the silence.

Angie took a sip of the iced tea that had just arrived. "I told you that Angelic says—"

"Mom, don't get me wrong, but I'm not backing out of this deal because some nutcase says my dead ancestors are unhappy with my decision." Jesse twirled the straw in between two fingers. "I may have acted rashly; I'll admit that. But who knows when this kind of opportunity will appear again. I had to act fast."

"And the fact that the gallery manager could be confused with a supermodel didn't factor into your decision at all, right? That's your story?"

"I didn't know she was the manager when I said yes to Rich. You know how important art is to me. I just wanted, I don't know, to be something besides a bull rider?" Jesse took off his ball cap and ran his fingers through his hair. He saw Taylor laugh at something her date said, and instantly Jesse went back to that moment in the studio when their gazes had connected. He'd felt so drawn to her.

A weekend out of town without risking the chance of running into Taylor DeMarco, that was what he needed. He'd have a clear head on Monday when he returned home.

Angie leaned back as the waitress set her plate of chicken and mushrooms in front of her. She waited for the waitress to deliver Jesse's T-bone, loaded baked, and side of Tex-Mex corn before she spoke again. "Angelic says the purchase will cause upheaval."

"I thought she drew the death card." Jesse cut into his steak, perfectly cooked to medium rare. He took a bite, and the juice ran into his mouth. The sensation made him glance across the street to Taylor. He watched as she flipped her head back and smiled, really smiled. No, the woman needed out of his head sooner than later. Now that he knew she was involved, that just made the mental switch easier.

"I've been thinking about that. The card doesn't have to mean an actual death. It could be the ending of a lifestyle, or maybe just represent the changeover of the gallery from their family to ours. Of course, we're not a rich, connected family like the Harrison/DeMarco group. Are you sure you're going to be able to keep the place going?" Angie cut her chicken into pieces as she chatted. She looked down at the plate and laughed. "I've been hanging out with the little ones too long. Look at what I did to my meat. I swear, those boys are changing my life even when I'm not playing Grandma Angie."

Jesse chuckled. "Maybe that was the life-changing event your fortune teller saw? You turning into a normal grandmother type."

"When hell freezes over," Angie said. "I hope I can represent you and the family appropriately tomorrow. You know, I tend to say what's on my mind."

Jesse took his mother's hand. "I wouldn't have it any other way. I need to know what I've gotten myself into before the sale is finalized. They've allowed me a two-week grace period to have my advisors look over the investment. You can spot a fraud faster than most people, even if you don't know a thing about art."

"Are you looking for a way out?" Angie twisted off a bottle cap and sipped the cold beer.

Jesse glanced over at the couple across the street, now eating their dinner. In his mind, he could see himself in the place of the man having dinner with Taylor. His mother was right—he had it bad. "Let's just see what's really going on there and we'll make a final decision in two weeks. I don't want to be swayed by the trappings."

His mom smiled and her words echoed in his head. "Sometimes fate brings you home."

Chapter 4

"The woman is crazy." Taylor glanced out her office door to see if her new BFF was within earshot. "I swear, she thinks she has to be glued to my side."

"I thought it was the cute bull rider who bought the gallery, not his mother." Brit sat on the leather couch, flipping through a portfolio. She reached the end of the book, closing it with a sigh. "I wish people wouldn't just drop these off. I can tell from the first two pages his art isn't up to show level yet. Maybe we could have a 'no portfolio' policy."

"I'm sure the new owner will want to implement a lot of new policies. You should bring it up with the two out there." Taylor pointed to the front where Angie stood talking to Barb. "They seem to be making plans already."

Brit laughed. "I haven't seen you this tweaked since that girl showed up unannounced at Ken's house during the senior party."

"Ugh, don't remind me. I made a complete and utter fool of myself that night." Taylor hadn't thought about her cheating, quarterback boyfriend for years. "She swore she didn't know he and I were even dating, let alone almost engaged. The jerk was playing her and me." She hated to think about Ken or Brad. Why was she so drawn to the bad boy? The man who couldn't commit to or love one just one person. Jesse Sullivan had a lot in common with her past boyfriends. He was handsome, charming, and a player. She wouldn't go down that road again.

"That's because you didn't put out like she did," Brit said. She opened another portfolio, carefully avoiding Taylor's eyes.

Taylor threw a pencil at her friend. "How do you know? Maybe I was a complete and utter slut with Ken?"

"Give me a break. Who was your best friend all during high school? You told me everything." Brit's smile widened. "Even that time you kissed the guy with the motorcycle at the dance in Kuna."

"One kiss is a lot different than what Ken was doing." Taylor leaned back in her chair. "How'd we get on this subject, anyway?"

"You started it."

"I did not." Taylor saw a flash of movement, and there in her office doorway stood Barbara Carico, Jesse Sullivan's manager and friend. Or were they more than friends? With Barb's wild red hair and slender body, a man would be a fool not to seal that deal. A stab of jealousy ran through Taylor's body. Why did she care who the bull rider felt attracted to? She stood and pasted on a smile. "Hey, anything I can help you with?"

Barb smiled a genuine smile, unlike the fake one plastered on Taylor's face. "Angie and I are heading out to grab some lunch. If you have time, we'd love to have you join us."

Taylor swallowed hard, pushing down the anger that gripped her. "I don't think so. I still have to finalize the sales from the showing."

Brit stood. "Go ahead, Taylor. I'll handle all that." She grabbed a file then leaned in close to Taylor and said, "Time to do some recon of your own."

Taylor stared at her friend, realizing the girl was right. What could it hurt to get to know these two a little better? Maybe she'd find a weak spot. One she could exploit before the two weeks expired. If Mr. Sullivan trusted these two, dropping a few false leads might work in her favor. She met Brit's gaze and nodded. "Thanks, Brit. Has Angie been to the tearoom over at The Bon? It's a perfect place for lunch."

"Actually, Angie has her heart set on going to Dave's," Barb said. "I guess they do a mean burger."

Taylor frowned. "The bar over on Fifth? I didn't realize they were still open, let alone serving lunch."

Brit looked like she was going to burst out laughing, and Taylor shot her a warning look.

"Angie knows the owner. I think they had a thing years ago when they both lived in Vegas." Barb smiled. "The woman knows more people than I do, especially men. Look, I know she can be a little grating, but she has a good heart. And she'd do anything for her boys."

Taylor focused on Barb's words. Was that a veiled warning? Telling her that the Sullivan boy was off-limits? The more she thought about this, the more she knew Brit was right. Time to find out what she was up against. Taylor grabbed her purse from the desk drawer and slung it over her coral pantsuit. Not exactly bar clothes, but it would have to do. "I'd love to have lunch with you."

She waved to Brit and walked outside with Barb. Angie stood waiting on the sidewalk with a half-smoked cigarette in her hand.

The woman blushed. "I'm working on stopping. It's just harder than I thought it would be."

Barb put her arm around the older woman. "No worries, I'm not going to rat you out." She glanced at Taylor and raised her eyebrows, urging the young gallery manager to agree.

"None of my business," Taylor said. She glanced down at her stacked platforms. "I should be good for the walk, unless you want to drive?"

"Heavens, no. We drive too much here." Angie stubbed out her cigarette in a flowerpot sitting by the gallery door. Taylor cringed.

If Sullivan took over the gallery they'd be selling authentic Indian headdresses and rodeo gear, and opening a beer bar in the back, sooner or later. She had to talk her folks out of this deal. Averting her eyes, she put on her best fake smile and brightly said, "Then we're off."

The inside of the bar was dark. Spilled beer, years of cigarette smoke, and grease from the kitchen assaulted Taylor as soon as she stepped inside. The three women sat in a booth. The red vinyl seats had turned brown from age, and the dark wood of the table was scratched and gnarled with use. Thankfully, someone had wiped it down before they arrived. A waitress or barmaid, Taylor wasn't sure what role the woman held, dropped off three menus and three plastic cups filled with water and ice.

"What can I get you to drink?" the woman asked. Taylor looked up, ready to order a glass of white wine. She stopped mid-order when she noticed a tattoo on the top exposed part of the woman's breast. It looked like ... No, it couldn't be. Taylor felt Angie's and Barb's gazes on her.

"Sheryl, show Taylor the rest of your tattoo," Angie said. "You'll love this."

The woman, Sheryl, grinned and leaned in closer. "You're not the first to notice. I got this last month." She pulled down her elastic neckline and Taylor was rewarded with the full view of a fully erect circumcised penis inked on the woman's breast. "My husband likes to tell people it's not at full scale, but he's fooling himself. The man isn't as well endowed as he thinks."

Taylor bit back a laugh. "Can I get a glass of white wine?"

Sheryl nodded, then listed off the available brands. Although they weren't the quality of wines the gallery carried at openings, they weren't that bad. Taylor ordered a dry chardonnay from Sun Valley winery, the same brand she kept at her house for *those* kind of days.

After Angie and Barb ordered their own drinks, beer and a large coke, Sheryl disappeared, promising to be right back.

"Sorry about the tattoo. Sheryl's pretty proud of it. She says her tips have tripled since she got inked." Angie grinned. "I bet you don't see that in the places you go."

Taylor laughed. "You're right about that. I don't think I've been in this bar since I was eighteen and trying not to get carded."

"Yeah, Gary had some issues with his bartenders when he took over the place. He had to put the fear of God into them. He's gotten rid of the few that wouldn't respect the law." Angie studied the menu.

"Gary?" Taylor asked.

"The owner."

"So his name's not Dave?" She glanced at the top of the menu.

Angie laughed. "Dave started the bar in the '70s. He was a great guy, fun loving, had a wicked sense of humor. Gary kept the name after he bought the place, kind of like a tribute."

Sheryl came back, dropped off their drinks, and took their lunch order. "Ten minutes, at the most. We're just like a chain place. You can get in and out in your thirty-minute lunch hour."

"And still get your beer," Barb added dryly when Sheryl was out of earshot. She held up her hands in mock surrender. "I know, I'm being a snob. But seriously, look at that guy over at the bar. You know he's been here since it opened this morning."

"Probably never left last night," Taylor added, turning to glance at the man. He wore jeans and a gray t-shirt, and had salt-and-pepper hair that stood up in random places on his head.

Angie sniffed. "You both are snobs. Nothing wrong with a man sitting at a bar all day. Maybe he's homeless and this is the only place he can sit."

Barb leaned into Angie and gave her a hug. "You're always looking for the best in people. I know; I shouldn't judge."

"I just think you need to be more open to the lost souls in the world." Angie's fingers drummed on the lacquered tabletop, diamond rings flashing in the glow cast from the neon sign lighting their table. Taylor took a long look at Angie. For all the bling around her neck and the bright yellow satin pants with matching floral-print shirt, the woman's words didn't match her sixties Barbie look.

"My mom would tell me the same thing," Taylor admitted. "My friends and I would go to the mall and laugh about someone's outfit, or the way they were dressed. But if my mom caught us, we knew we were in trouble. One day she took us to the rescue mission, and we served lunch for a week."

"Sounds like your mother raised you right." Angie nodded.

Taylor tilted her head. "Did you do the same thing to Jesse when he was a kid?"

Angie's face paled and tears filled her eyes. Taylor froze. What had she said?

Finally Barb spoke up. "Angie didn't raise the boys. They lived with their dad." Her quiet voice told Taylor there was much more to the story.

"Oh." Taylor dug into her purse and handed Angie a tissue. "I didn't mean to be too personal."

Angie took the tissue and waved away Taylor's apology. "No worries. My issues." She blew her nose. "Barb went to school with James and Jesse in Shawnee. They were all friends."

Taylor focused on Barb. "Shawnee? Does that place even have a school?"

"Hey, it's not that small. Okay, it's not big like Boise, but yes, Shawnee had three schools: elementary, middle, and high school. I was friends with Lizzie, who dated James. Therefore, Jesse tagged along, too. We've been friends for years."

Taylor thought about Brit, who she'd met freshman year at Bishop Kelly. "My assistant and I went to high school together. She understands me."

"Yeah, I get that. Lizzie was the only one I could talk to when my husband and I started having problems." Barb twisted the ring on her left hand. Taylor hadn't noticed it there before.

Angie huffed. "No, Lizzie was the only one you told. You have to realize that once you're in the Sullivan fold, you have family. We may be unusual, but we're family."

Barb laughed. "Jesse came over the day I signed the annulment papers. He watched *Sleepless in Seattle* with me for hours. I drank three bottles of wine that night."

"Wait, the annulment?" Taylor was confused.

"Long story. Let's just say, Hunter and I have been through some intense times. I tell him we should get that Chinese curse tattooed on our shoulders, the one that says 'may your lives be interesting.'" Barb leaned back as Sheryl delivered the food.

The smell of French fries and grease filled Taylor's senses, and her stomach growled. "I haven't had a burger in years. Usually, we order sandwiches for lunch, and then I have a salad for dinner when I get home. My folks are gone a lot—either for work or traveling—so, I've been on my own."

Angie smiled. "You live at home then? I keep telling Jesse that it's not unusual for an unmarried child to live with his parent. But he keeps telling me I need my own house when I'm in town. I've been looking at one of those condos over by the river."

Taylor brightened. "Me, too. I thought, once the gallery gets settled in a year or two, I should be able to—" She cut off her thought, realizing that if Jesse continued with his plans to buy the gallery, her dream would be out of reach. If that happened, she'd have to dip into her trust fund or ask her parents for money to get her condo. Those were two things she didn't want to do.

The table grew quiet as the impact of Taylor's words hit the ladies. The women focused on their food, and all casual conversation stopped. *Great*, Taylor thought. *Way to alienate friends and influence people.*

A man's hand reached in and grabbed a couple of her fries. She slapped at it. "Hey!"

Jesse Sullivan slipped in to the booth next to her. Heat coursed through her body and pooled in the spot between her legs. Damn him and his crooked smile.

"Sorry, they just looked too inviting. Besides, you can't eat fries, not with that body." Jesse half stood, leaning over the table to give his mother a kiss on the cheek.

Sheryl returned to the table. "The usual, Jesse?"

"Sounds good. Make sure the hot wings are really hot this time." Jesse took a swig of the draft beer Sheryl had brought without asking. Apparently, the man and his mother were regulars.

"Who invited you?" Barb asked, pointing a fry at the newcomer.

Jesse leaned back in the booth and smiled at his manager. "Now, Barbie, why are you being a brat? It's not like I crashed your wedding, or something."

"Boy, you're always showing up at the wrong time." Barb grinned. "Hunter's still peeved at you crashing in my hotel room the night after our first wedding. Every time we leave for a rodeo, he checks to see if you have your own hotel reservation."

"He's just doing his due diligence as the doting husband. Besides, I know not to touch sold goods. I get beaten up enough on the bulls; no way I want some angry husband messing with this pretty face." Jesse ran his hand over his chin.

"The face that didn't get shaved this morning," Angie observed.

Jesse leaned over to Taylor. "Now you understand why I sent these two over to the gallery this morning. If they're all up in your business, maybe they'll stay out of mine."

"Jesse." Angie shook her finger at her youngest son. "You stop being a brat." She frowned at the plate of chicken wings Sheryl just sat down in front of him. "Lord, do those things smell."

"Like heaven." Jesse smiled and ripped into a wing. The smell of Tabasco hit Taylor, and she coughed.

"Wow." She took a sip of her wine. "I'm not even eating them and I can taste the hot sauce."

Grinning, Jesse waved a drumlet near her. "I know, aren't they amazing?"

Angie laughed. "Better get used to it, Taylor. Now that you're part of the gang, Jesse's eating habits are one thing you just have to ignore."

Taylor smiled, but deep down she wondered if she was really part of the gang. How had this family accepted her so quickly as a friend when she was working as hard as she could to get them out of her life?

"Relax, Mom. Maybe Taylor's looking for the exit door instead of being brainwashed into our little cult." Jesse wiped his mouth with a paper napkin. "Mom, I mean, Angie, has this habit of moving too quickly in her relationships. If you don't watch out, pretty soon she'll be mother-henning you, too. And you'll be one of the family, like it or not."

Taylor ate her lunch and wondered why the prospect didn't seem like such a bad idea.

Chapter 5

Jesse walked through the gallery alone. Yesterday's lunch had gone long, and the three women had acted like best friends before they'd left Dave's. The dark, old, dive bar had been the last place he thought prissy Miss Taylor would agree to eat. His mom had that effect on everyone, though. The ability to break down class barriers. He wondered how Susan and her husband would react to the Angie experience.

Standing in front of a modernist take on a landscape, Jesse found himself not thinking about the angles of the painting. Instead, he thought about the angles of Taylor's face. He'd worked on the drawing of her for the last week, trying to find the missing spark, the look he saw every time their eyes met. But his skill level had failed him, and he'd started over time and time again, frustrated with the results. Three weeks and this semester would be over. Would Susan agree to keep him on as a private student, even though he was taking over the gallery? Was there some sort of conflict in the two items? He hoped not. Besides, if everything worked out, he'd be more of a silent owner for the next few years, allowing Taylor to stay on and manage the gallery.

If she agreed.

He stepped to the next painting, trying to focus on the technique. But his mind returned to Taylor. Maybe Angie was right. Maybe he was drawn more to the woman than the actual business. If Taylor wouldn't stay he'd just hire a new gallery manager. Angie didn't want to take over the business. She'd agreed to share the open receptionist position that a college student on summer break currently held. Angie didn't love art, not the way Taylor did. Or the way a gallery manager should, he corrected himself. The gallery manager didn't have to be Taylor. His lips curled into a smile. It would just be a bonus if she stayed on.

As if his thoughts had made her materialize, the girl he couldn't capture on paper walked out of her office. With the suit behind her. The same man she'd had dinner with on Tuesday. Today, she wore a sleeveless summer shift dress that showed off her well-toned arms. No wonder the man kept showing up. He was marking his territory, Jesse guessed. She walked the man to the door, then turned and spotted Jesse standing in the gallery. The girl had the grace to flush.

She strolled toward him, and he could see her processing her thoughts as she made her way over. She nodded to the painting. "Nora Wilson is the artist. She sells well here. You'll probably want to keep her happy if you take over."

Jesse cocked his head. "Don't you mean when?"

Taylor flushed a beet red. "Yes, of course. Sorry for the poor choice of words." She glanced at her watch. "I'm late for an appointment. Busy day." She started to step away.

"I was hoping I could shadow you today." His words stopped her forward movement.

Turning, she frowned. "I thought Angie and Barb were doing that yesterday."

Jesse leaned against the wall, watching her. "It's a big investment. I'd like to know what I'm buying."

She arched a brow at him. "How will shadowing me help?"

"You're the manager. The manager knows everything. Just ask Barb." He let his gaze drop to her suntanned legs. Damn, the woman didn't have a flaw on her body. *Or at least the parts of her body you've seen.* He inwardly shivered at the thought. He slowly brought his gaze back up to her face. His attention had been noticed, and now there was a hardness in her eyes. She was angry with him. Probably for making her feel something after her suit of a boyfriend had just left. Oh, well.

He watched her consider his request. Finally, he saw her surrender, and she sighed, verbalizing it. "Fine, I'm driving out to Baker City to meet with a potential artist. You sure you want to be stuck in a car for that long?

With you? Anytime.

"I'll even drive."

She stopped in her office to grab her purse and let Brit know they were leaving. The assistant smiled and waved at him like she thought they were going on a date, not a business drive. He wished. Taylor frowned at the girl as they left.

As they left the gallery, Taylor slipped on a pair of sunglasses, hiding her eyes. He nodded to the Porsche sitting in the parking lot to the side of the gallery. A 1985, 944 model, the baby was his pride and joy. He'd bought the thing for pennies and had put thousands into restoring the car to its former glory. Candy apple red, the car got its share of looks when he took it out for a drive.

"Flashy," Taylor admitted. "And so not what I expected. My father would kill you for this car."

"You should have seen it when I bought it. James told me I was out of my mind. That finding the parts alone would ruin me." He held the passenger door open for her, watching as she slipped in. Her long, elegant legs were the last part of her body to disappear into the Porsche.

When he climbed into the driver's side, he turned the keys, letting the engine sing. A smile tickled his lips. The car made him happy. He wasn't proud of the fact, but it did.

"So, you had to prove your brother wrong?" Taylor questioned.

"No. Well, maybe. James is James. As the older brother, he has an opinion on everything." Jesse turned to Taylor. "I love the car, but James was right about one thing. It ran me an arm and a leg to restore her. I just make sure he doesn't know how much."

"Angie said the two of you grew up with your dad. That must have been fun—living out in the country like that. Is that where you learned to ride bulls? Did your dad teach you?" Taylor pulled a slip of paper from her purse and handed it to him. "Key this into your GPS, it's the guy's address."

Jesse typed the address into the navigator he'd had installed. When the map pulled up, he frowned. "Two hours, thirty minutes? You're going to have to feed me lunch and dinner."

Taylor laughed. "Who said anything about food?"

"I am driving, the least you can do is feed me." Jesse pulled the car out into traffic, adjusting the rearview mirror. From his peripheral vision, he saw Taylor turning her head toward the gallery, watching it like they were leaving forever.

"That can be arranged," she finally said after they'd turned the corner, and the building was no longer in sight.

They reached the freeway and headed east before he answered her questions. "I'm surprised Angie said anything about Dad. She likes to pretend all that didn't happen."

"I don't understand." Taylor turned down the stereo. "She doesn't like to talk about her divorce?"

Jesse turned his head and looked at her. "She didn't tell you, did she?"

"Tell me what?"

Jesse wondered if he even wanted Taylor to know about his sordid past. He sped up to pass a minivan that was slowing for the exit to Eagle, using the distraction to think. He considered his options. "Look, you can't tell Angie I told you this. If she wants you to know, you'll know. But it's hard for her to admit what she did, and I don't want her hurt."

Taylor held her hands up. "I'm not going to hurt Angie. Or at least, I hope not. I don't know what I said yesterday, but she teared up on me. So what really happened?"

Jesse glanced at the GPS. Seeing he didn't have a turnoff to worry about for miles, he decided to let her in. "When James and I were kids, Angie left Dad."

"They got a divorce. It happens in the best of families, believe me." Taylor checked her cell phone for messages. "Most of my senior class was playing the two-step home game, one week at mom's, one at dad's. I could never find anyone."

"No, well, yeah, they got a divorce, but we didn't know that. One day we had a mother, the next we didn't. Dad wouldn't talk about it. He wouldn't let us talk about her. We were just kids— James must have been six, me a year younger. Once she was gone, Dad fell apart, and raising me fell on James." Jesse paused. "Then Dad died a few years ago while he was on the way to one of my rodeos. The police found an empty flask in the truck when they pulled him out of the river."

Taylor didn't say anything. Jesse glanced over at her, wondering what she was reading on her cell. Instead, her gaze was focused on him, her eyes wide.

She bit her bottom lip. "No wonder she acted funny. I'm so sorry, Jesse. I didn't know."

"I'm okay. James is okay. But Mom, she likes to be called Angie, even by us. She's kind of a mess about it." Jesse stared at the road ahead. "I think she regretted leaving as soon as she got out of town, but Dad wouldn't even let her talk to us. Hell, for years, James and I assumed she'd died somewhere along the way."

"How did you find her?" Taylor's voice was quiet.

"She'd been following me on the rodeo circuit. Believe it or not, Jesse Sullivan isn't that common of a name." Jesse grinned. "One day, after a ride, she showed up at a bar where I'd been celebrating. James had already turned in for the night."

"What, she came up and said, 'Hi, I'm your mother'?"

"Kind of. I thought she was a kook. Then we got talking and she knew too much. She had a picture of the four of us, taken just before she left." Jesse turned on the air conditioner. "After that, I wasn't an orphan anymore. She's an interesting mom, that's for sure, but I'm glad I have her."

"Did James feel the same way?" Taylor asked.

"Not hardly. He's struggled with the idea. But Lizzie's helping, and Angie loves the kids." Jesse paused. "I think he remembers the life we had before she left. And he missed her too much to just forgive a whim."

"Of all the things you could have told me about your mother, about your family, really, this wasn't what I expected." Taylor put her hand on his arm. "Thanks."

Jesse pursed his lips together. "Well, I wouldn't have said anything, but Angie is kind of hard to accept if you don't know the background. She's got her heart set on this receptionist thing."

Taylor laughed. "I know, she was trying it out yesterday afternoon. I think she scared away more customers than came in."

"Sorry about that. Maybe you or Barb can take her shopping for work-appropriate clothes. Stuff that shows a little less cleavage?" Jesse grimaced. "I can't believe I'm saying this about my mother. You're lucky; Susan doesn't embarrass you."

"Oh, if you only knew." Taylor laughed. "Imagine being the kid whose mom brought paintings in for career day with nude models. The boys were always asking if I wanted to go play artist."

Jesse's mouth turned up in one corner. "So I won't get to first base by asking if you want to see my sketches?"

"You may get a knee to the groin, à la two years of self-defense classes." Taylor focused on the farmland outside the window.

But I really do have sketches, he thought. *Would Taylor think I was a psycho if she ever saw the studies I've completed? One after another, trying to get the arch of her cheekbone just right. Or the line of her nose.* They were both silent for a while.

She laughed. "Family can really mess with your head, you know?"

Jesse smiled. "We have a lot in common, you and me. A lot in common."

• • •

Taylor watched Jesse as he listened to the artist talk about the paintings they'd come to preview. The two men talked color, line, and light, like they'd been studying together for years. She had to admit, she was impressed. For a bull rider, the man knew his stuff about art. She'd been trying to sign Marvin to a show for years. He'd always put her off, claiming he just wasn't ready. She'd lost count of the number of times she'd driven out here, her hopes high on the drive to Oregon and depressed on the way home. Jesse not only had the artist's signature on the contract, the man had agreed to do four exclusive projects for the show. Now the two were settling on a theme.

She should feel happy. But all she could see was the gallery slipping away from her. Mike had been clear: there wasn't a legal leg to stand on for her to challenge her parents' sale of the gallery. Her grandfather had left the business solely in the hands of his one and only daughter. Not daughter *and* granddaughter. But that's what she knew her grandpa had wanted. For Main Street to be passed down to her when the time came. That's why she'd worked so hard to bring in new talent, new buyers. She'd even started a web page for the company. Now Mr. Charming over there would reap the rewards of her hard work, and she'd be relegated down to employee status. Not owner. Her grandfather wanted her to take over the gallery, and she wouldn't let him down. Not just because Jesse wanted to play artist.

Taylor wasn't sure if that's what frustrated her the most—the title. She knew the money wasn't the issue; she'd been assured her inheritance would be substantial. And if she needed money she could always turn to the trust her grandfather left her. But everything couldn't be about money, could it? What about family tradition? What about—she searched for the right word—power? *Maybe,* she thought, *maybe I'm worried about losing my status in the art community.* She shook her head and turned back to the two men discussing artwork.

She knew she should participate in the conversation, but she had decided on the way here that Jesse Sullivan needed a taste of what he was buying. She wanted him to feel the pain of trying to sign an artist who so desperately needed to be showcased, only to be turned away. Yet, Jesse hadn't been turned away. Instead, Marvin had welcomed him like a long lost brother. She wanted to think she'd softened him up the last few years. But it was Jesse who had worked his magic. And she'd have to swallow her pride and let him know he'd done a good, no, great job today. Even if the words choked her like the fast food hamburger they'd be having on the way home.

Jesse looked over at her and smiled, making a thumbs-up gesture when Marvin turned his back. The guy was having fun. And she was the one who set him up for success.

She was doomed.

Thirty minutes later they were on their way back to Boise with Marvin's portfolio on the back seat.

"So we can set up a show date now and get the paintings shipped?" Jesse asked.

"Not until we finalize the contract. It has to go to Mike, our lawyer, first. He checks out all the legal stuff then sends a formal copy back to Marvin. I guess we'll have to figure out who is signing—you or my dad. I don't know if you want to be fettered to a contract you didn't vet." She looked at him. "Besides, I did all of the leg work; the contract should be considered my product."

"I don't know, he didn't seem very interested until I started talking. Besides, your lawyer or mine, it's all the same. They all just want to be paid," Jesse said. "But you're right; we probably better decide if this is a pre-sale item or something to happen afterward." Jesse glanced over at her. "You a betting kind of girl?"

"I don't understand." A headache was blooming in the back of her skull. Probably karma for trying to keep Jesse from knowing she was trying to outbid him for the gallery. She never had been a good liar. Taylor reached back and massaged her neck. Maybe an appointment at the spa wouldn't be a bad idea.

Jesse pulled the car onto the exit ramp leading toward Ontario. Ontario was the first town in Oregon that they'd passed heading in to meet with Marvin. It was the last town in Oregon they were going to pass on their way back to Idaho.

"What are you doing?" Taylor closed her eyes. All she wanted to do was to go home. She could open a bottle of wine and sit in the hot tub on her deck. Alone. Without the hunk of a bull rider playing games with her.

"You're buying me lunch. There's a great steakhouse here in town. And, since it's late for lunch, early for dinner, I'll take one meal for the two you owe me." Jesse slowed the car to a stop at the light. When it turned green, he pulled onto the main street of town. "And I think we can determine who gets credit for Marvin's contract at the same time."

"I still don't understand." Taylor's stomach growled at the thought of food. She wasn't going to argue. Besides, he was driving.

"You'll see after we eat." Jesse grinned. "I just want to warn you, I'm kind of a big thing here."

"My God. You have such an ego." Taylor shook her head. She instantly regretted the motion and reached into her purse for the bottle of pain reliever she kept for moments like this. She shook out two pills, then washed them down with the rest of her water. She threw the empty water bottle onto the back seat.

"Just go ahead and make yourself at home," Jesse said.

Taylor closed her eyes and prayed for the pills to take effect. "I'll get it when we stop for dinner. I promise I'm not going to trash your pretty car."

"Better not, or I'll stop taking you places." Jesse's voice sounded far away and Taylor realized she could easily fall asleep if she had half a second.

Chapter 6

The warmth of a hand on her shoulder caused Taylor to turn. Had the car stopped? Jesse stood outside her open door. She wiped her hand over her eyes. "Sorry. Must have fallen asleep."

"You think? Come on, Sleeping Beauty, let's get that dinner you promised me." Jesse pulled her out of the car and they walked into the old building. The outside looked more like the Wild West than a modern steakhouse. She glanced at the pair of rockers sitting on the wooden deck—a checkers game sat forgotten between the oak chairs.

"Where are we?" She stopped in the middle of the porch, glancing at the old metal signs on the wall. The place looked like it hadn't been open in years. Momentarily, fear flitted through her mind. Was she being stupid? What did she really know about Jesse Sullivan, besides the fact that her mom liked the guy? Her mom didn't have the best radar for freaks. Had the road trip been a mistake? She felt in her purse for her cell.

"Relax, I'm not leading you astray. Yet." Somehow the man seemed to know what she was thinking before she opened her mouth. Jesse put a hand on the small of her back and eased her through the black-painted glass doors.

As soon as they entered, the sound of an old song filled her ears and tickled at her memory. Was that Patsy Cline or a newish version of the song by that teenaged wonder kid? "Blue," that was the song name, and the woman's voice crooned over the mostly-empty dining room. A wooden bar complete with mirrored shelves and liquor bottles graced the left side of the room. On the right, a dance floor sat next to a small, darkened stage.

"Jesse Sullivan, what are you doing in town? I know there isn't a rodeo this week," a rough female voice called out from behind the bar. Jesse turned them toward the voice.

"Maggie, this is Taylor." Jesse leaned over the bar and kissed the older woman on the cheek. "How have you been? George still giving you a hard time?"

"That ex-husband of mine should be drawn and quartered. But he's been out of town on a job site the last few months, so it's easier just to avoid his calls." Maggie nodded at Taylor. "How'd this rangy old cowboy talk you into being seen with him? You're a beautiful girl, I'm sure you could do better."

Jesse put his hand on his chest and faked recoil from the shot. "You're breaking my heart, Maggie. Why do you have to treat me so badly?"

Maggie laughed. It was a harsh sound made deeper from, what Taylor could imagine, years of breathing in the smoke from bar patrons. If the woman didn't indulge in cigarettes herself. "I'm on a crusade to make sure that the women you date know the whole story, Jesse Sullivan, not just the fairy tale you spin." She turned her focus back to Taylor, flipping a clean white bar towel over her shoulder. Her eyes narrowed and Taylor felt the steel behind the woman's gaze, sizing her up even as she kept her words light and friendly. "I can't count the number of hearts this boy has broken in this town alone."

"You make me sound like a gigolo. I can't help it if they get the wrong idea when I'm nice to someone." He nodded toward the dining room. "Too early to get some food? The woman's a slave driver. I haven't eaten since breakfast."

Taylor slapped his arm. "Hey, I didn't even ask you to come along, you invited yourself."

"Now, why doesn't that surprise me?" Maggie's voice had a distinct drawl, and Taylor wondered if the Pacific Northwest wasn't the woman's first home. Was that a hint of Texas twang in her voice?

Jesse held his hands up in mock surrender. "I give up. Having two of you attacking me just isn't fair."

"Poor, misunderstood bull rider," Maggie quipped. She pointed to a table near the dance floor. "Go sit, and I'll send one of the girls out to get your order. Can I pull you something from the bar?"

"Two drafts?" Jesse glanced at Taylor. "Unless you'd like something different?"

Taylor shrugged, realizing her headache had disappeared during the short nap. "As long as it's light, draft is fine."

Jesse slapped his stomach. "I have to watch my girlish figure."

Shaking her head, Taylor smiled at Maggie. "It was nice to meet you."

"Just keep the boy in line; that's all the advice I can give you." Maggie reached for the chilled glasses. "Get settled. I'll bring these over in a second."

"You know I'm right here and can hear you, right?" Jesse shrugged. "Come on, Taylor, we've been dismissed."

He took her arm and led her to the table farthest away from the bar. He raised his voice and said, "Maggie can't eavesdrop on us all the way over here."

"You're not all that interesting, bull rider," Maggie called back.

He chuckled as he held out a chair for Taylor. "The woman loves me; what can I say. I told you I was kind of a big deal here."

"I think you overestimate your charm, Mr. Sullivan," Taylor said.

Jesse sat across from her, the table small enough that she could feel the heat from his legs so close to her own. He flashed what she'd come to think of as his promotional smile. "I think you protest too much."

A waitress slapped two glasses of water on the table along with two menus. "Hi, Jesse."

"Hey, Amanda." Jesse didn't even look at the girl. Taylor could feel the jealousy flowing from the waitress. "Can you bring us an order of wings?"

"Whatever." The girl stomped off.

Taylor watched her bang through the kitchen door. "One of your exes?"

Jesse leaned back, running his hand through his hair. "That's Maggie's daughter. She's way too young, but boy, the girl is determined." He lifted his eyebrows. "You really got her in a snit."

"Me? What did I do?" Taylor looked up from the menu and found Jesse staring.

He reached out and pushed a wayward lock of hair off her shoulder. "You came in with me."

Taylor could feel the blush heat her cheeks, even as she willed it away. She was not interested in Jesse Sullivan, not in that way. Not now, not ever. He was her future employer, that's all. And if she had her way, he wouldn't even be that. Mike's call that morning had made her realize she needed to be proactive. Maybe even buy the gallery herself? If she cashed out the available funds from the trust fund her grandfather set up, she'd still have to borrow heavily. The thought of that much debt turned her stomach, and she pushed away the menu.

"Not hungry?" Jesse stared at her like she had spoken.

"I just know what I want." She smiled as his eyes widened a bit at the statement. Time to break his heart. Or dampen his ego just a bit. "Cheeseburger and fries."

"Not what I thought you were going to say." Jesse turned his attention back to the menu. "I figured you'd go for the rib-eye dinner."

"I could be persuaded, if I wasn't paying. Or, if the gallery wasn't paying," she corrected herself. "We have a policy of limiting meals to a fifteen dollar max, except for potential clients and artists. And you are neither. Welcome to the world of corporate art."

"You just want me to buy you dinner." Jesse shook his head. "Pitiful how low a girl will stoop to be a part of the Jesse show."

The waitress returned, still throwing mooning looks at Jesse and hate-filled glances at Taylor. Jesse sighed. "I have to buy, just so you can experience the joy that a steak from Maggie's brings."

Taylor brightened, opening the menu. "In that case, I'll have the rib-eye and lobster, steamed veggies over the fettuccini pasta, and a side salad with light Italian on the side."

"Ouch." Jesse faked a heart attack. "You know how to hit a guy where it hurts."

Taylor arched an eyebrow. "The wallet?"

Jesse nodded and ordered his own steak. "Bring us two more drafts while you're at it."

The girl spun on her booted heel and left the table. Taylor watched her stop by the bar to leave the drink order with her mother before disappearing into the kitchen.

"Do you think I should hire a food taster before I eat?" Taylor stared at the swinging kitchen door. She hadn't felt a girl's hatred that intense since high school. Tom, the school bad boy, had dropped his long-term, stoner girlfriend and started calling Taylor instead. Coincidentally, that particular bad boy was a gifted artist who hadn't had a clue. He had later admitted that he'd needed Taylor to introduce him to her grandfather.

Tom still used the gallery to sell his landscapes. He was developing quite a following and had even been interviewed by several local magazines. He hadn't broken in yet, but Taylor knew it was only a matter of time. The guy was good. Very good.

She looked at Jesse, and for a second, she could see what the waitress saw in him. The guy was nice, sensitive, and not bad looking. If he didn't have an ego the size of undeveloped Canada, he might even be date-worthy. She shook her head. Jesse Sullivan was the enemy. And this was the best shot she'd have to get intel on the guy. She grinned, thinking of herself as a secret spy, and wondered if the beer was clouding her judgment a tiny bit. She decided she didn't really care and took another drink.

While they ate their dinner, Jesse kept her entertained with stories from the road. Riders who'd shown up for their ride after a desperate search for their lucky rope. Or their lucky bandana. "Riders are a superstitious bunch. None of them own a black cat or would step on a crack on a bet. The life has its risks; pretending that the danger can be staved off with luck is a coping mechanism."

"You're smart," she said, regretting the compliment as soon as it left her mouth. She ducked her head and asked another question. "What are your superstitions?"

"Can't tell you." He cut one last piece off his steak before he pushed the plate away.

Taylor leaned forward. Now this was getting interesting. "Why not?"

"If I tell you, they lose their magic." Jesse actually blushed. "Look, I know it's dumb, but it's kind of like telling your birthday wish after you blow out your candles. It's just not done."

"I would never have pegged you as a woo-woo guy." She finished off her last bites and leaned back and groaned. "I'm going to have to buy all new pants. I think I just gained ten pounds while sitting here."

Maggie came by the table to clear the plates. "That's the best compliment we've had in years. I'll tell Duke you enjoyed your meal."

"Duke?" Taylor cocked her head and watched Maggie.

Maggie's eyes were soft as she said, "My husband. He's our cook."

"And an ex-champion bull rider, himself. The man is a legend. The bulls he rode during the day, well, he was the only one who could stay on Satin, ever. They had to retire the bull after Duke retired. The bull riding association didn't think it would be suitable for someone else to master the bull because of its aging body." Jesse's hands flew all over the place when he was excited and telling a story.

"Wait, the bull's name was Satin?" Taylor had no clue on the proper names for bulls in the business, but Satin? That sounded like a kitten.

Jesse laughed. "His black coat was as smooth as silk and riders just slipped off him."

"And now Duke cooks here. No wonder you wanted to come me to come with you." Taylor smiled at Maggie. "Be sure to tell your husband how much I enjoyed dinner."

"I'll tell him you're here." Maggie put a hand on Jesse's shoulder. "He'll sure be glad to see you. You heading out to Wyoming this weekend?"

"Yep. I've got three more months I promised Barb I'd ride. Then I'm done for the year. Well, unless I get into the finals. Which would mean I'd have to take one last ride." Jesse sounded unsure, almost hesitant.

"It's for the best. You've about used up your lucky-charm points, you realize that, right?" Maggie nodded to the empty glasses. "Why don't I bring you over a pitcher?"

"Oh, I think we're about done," Taylor said at the same time as Jesse nodded.

He grinned at her. "We still haven't ironed out the details of who gets credit for the contract we signed this afternoon." He stood and spoke to Maggie. "Bring the pitcher over to the dart board. Is my dart case still under the bar?"

"Of course." Maggie nodded at Taylor. "I'll bring you a good set, too. If you have a chance against this guy it won't be with house darts." Then she disappeared into the back room.

"Why do I feel like the two of you are speaking a foreign language? What the heck are house darts?" Taylor followed Jesse deeper into the bar. They stopped in front of three flashing, soft-tip dartboards. On the floor lay a piece of vinyl marking the throw line. Taylor pointed to the neon orange strip. "Where's the women's tee?"

Jesse pressed his lips together, trying to suppress a laugh, but Taylor saw it.

"What dumb thing did I say now?" Taylor set her purse on the floor next to a table where Jesse had laid out a handful of quarters and his beer glass. She drained her glass and set it on the table as well.

"You're thinking about golf. There's not a shorter throw line for women." He cocked his head and looked at her. "Unless you're just playing me? No way you could have gotten out of college without playing one game of darts at a local dive bar."

"I don't know where you went to school, but my college days were filled with hours in the library museum studying the masters."

Maggie set a case down on the table for Jesse and handed Taylor a set of heavy darts. In her other hand she held a set of three neon-yellow plastic darts that she held up for Taylor to see.

"These are house darts." Maggie handed them to Taylor. "Take one and compare the weight with the others."

Taylor felt the light, cheap plastic dart. She looked at Maggie. "So heavier is better?"

Jesse held out his own darts, and Taylor took one, comparing it to the other two. She glanced up, frowning. He grinned. "It depends on the thrower. My darts are almost as light as house darts, even though they're titanium."

"And pricey as hell," Maggie added. "You don't know how many people I have to take that case away from. I think you should consider taking it home with you."

"I don't play anywhere but here." Jesse took the dart back and walked up to the line. He leaned his body over the vinyl tape, reached out his arm and threw his first dart. It landed just outside the bull's-eye.

Taylor watched as he adjusted his stance. Jesse lined up his body so his right shoulder was parallel to the bull's-eye on the board. By the third dart, he'd hit his target. Crap, what had she gotten herself into?

She handed the house dart back to Maggie with a slight smile. "I guess I better get practicing."

Maggie watched Jesse throw another three darts. "My money's on you. Jesse's a great player when his head's in the game. But I think he's got something else on his mind tonight." She grinned at Taylor. "Nice to meet you. I hope you come back, with or without that one."

"I hear you," Jesse called out from the line, continuing to throw.

Taylor poured a fresh glass of beer from the pitcher Maggie had brought. "I just might have to do that."

They threw darts for over ten minutes before Jesse stopped and returned to the table. He poured himself another beer and watched her for a while.

Conscious of his eyes on her, Taylor tried to focus on the way the dart felt when it left her hand. She thought about where she wanted it to land. Not too hard, not too soft, the power behind the dart had to be just right to keep it flying in the direction of the intended target. Finally, she returned to the table, laying her darts down to take a sip from her glass.

"You're good," Jesse said. "So I guess I was right about the college dive bar obsession."

"No. Like I said, in college I focused on studying. It was after I graduated that I fell in love with dive bars."

"That's my girl." Jesse smiled. Her heart was beating too fast. The bar suddenly felt hot. Had he meant the words, or was that a casual throwaway line for Jesse the heartbreaker? He continued before she could say anything. "Now about that wager."

"When did we say we were playing darts to settle this?"

Jesse glanced around the bar. "Shuffleboard, pool, or Hunter's Gallery?"

Taylor followed his gaze. She'd never shot a gun in her life, real or virtual. Shuffleboard seemed, well, just wrong. And pool, she knew she totally sucked there. "Fine, darts. But we need rules."

"I win three out of five games, and you sleep with me." Jesse toyed with the quarters.

"What did you say?" Taylor couldn't breathe.

He grinned his million-dollar smile that Taylor bet worked on most women. "Just seeing if you were paying attention." He leaned closer. "Rules. Three out of five, winner of each game goes first, loser chooses the game. Winner at the end gets credit for the contract."

Taylor hesitated, wondering just how good Jesse was at this game. Maybe she should laugh his idea off and offer to share the credit. She watched him continue to juggle the quarters. "Winner of each game buys the drinks."

His eyes widened—she'd surprised him. That could work in her favor. She nodded to the board. "Go set it up and let's get this match started."

She won the first game, surprising both herself and Jesse. For her first win, she ordered two shots of cinnamon firewater, a drink her father had bought her when she'd turned of-age. No one could handle the burn unless they'd been indoctrinated into the firewater family. She'd surprised him again with the order. She was definitely keeping the boy on his toes.

When he won the second game, Taylor wasn't surprised. She should have seen Jesse's tequila shot order as a warning sign. However, the beer and firewater had already dulled the part of her brain screaming at her that this was a terrible idea.

He looked smug when she chose Cricket, a game where you had to hit your target. He must have thought that's why he was winning. Taylor knew better; she was just warming up. She'd been less than honest about her dart history, but he didn't need to know that.

When she won game three, he stood motionless, staring at her. "You've played before," he said.

Shrugging, she ordered another firewater shot.

He tapped her hand. "You keep a lot of secrets, you know."

She watched him shoot the drink, slamming the empty glass upside down on the tray. *Buddy, you have no idea.*

Chapter 7

Two hours later, they stumbled into the back of a taxi Maggie had called to take them to a local hotel. "Take us somewhere that has late-night room service."

The man in the front laughed. "Do you know where you are? Ontario's not a big city. Besides, with the livestock show in town, Maggie was lucky to get you a room anywhere."

"Maggie got us a room?" Jesse's head hurt trying to follow the taxi driver's words. He never felt alcohol. Of course, he'd never mixed firewater with tequila before. Taylor twisted him in more ways than he cared to admit. She confused him. Especially when she laid her head on his shoulder after they got into the cab. Her blond hair tickled his cheek, and the floral smell of her hair flooded his senses. Food, they needed food.

"Two rooms. She got us two rooms, right?" Taylor murmured from his chest, apparently still alive.

He smiled at her drunken defiance. The girl had backbone, that much was obvious. "Can we stop by a drive-in on the way to the motel?"

"Best burgers in town up ahead on your right. Will that work?" The taxi driver looked at him in the rearview. Jesse saw his eyes drop to Taylor in an appreciative glance.

Why wasn't this girl dating, engaged, or hell, even married off? Jesse couldn't imagine. Then Angie's voice echoed in his head when he complained about everyone hooking up around him. "You're just waiting for the one." Maybe that was Taylor's problem, too. She hadn't found the one. He turned his focus back to the driver. "Works for me."

The car slowed as they pulled into the drive-through, and the driver inched the car forward so Jesse could order. "A monster cheeseburger with bacon." He stopped when Taylor lifted her head.

"Two. With curly fries. And a large coke," she mumbled to herself and laid her head back down.

Jesse smiled and repeated the order into the speaker. He pulled his wallet out and paid for the food. The smell of grease and beef made his stomach growl as soon as the server handed him a large bag.

Taylor lifted her head and shifted in her seat in order to take a drink from one of the cups. A loud burp seemed to surprise her when it followed. "God, don't let me drink with you again. Can't you ever let someone win?"

Jesse opened the bag and offered her a fry. She grabbed a handful, glancing around the dark streets. "Where are we going?"

The driver answered her. "Cowboy's Bunk Motel over on King Street. Maggie knows the owner."

Jesse glanced at the taxi driver's posted license for a name. "Todd, you seem to know a lot about Maggie."

The kid, in his early twenties, blushed. "I kind of hang out there when I'm not driving."

Jesse wondered if the kid hung out for the food or to see Amanda. He'd bet from the reaction, it was Amanda.

In less than five minutes, they were at the motel. Jesse helped Taylor out of the cab and paid Todd, adding in a hefty tip. The older woman at the desk turned down the television she'd been watching. "You must be Jesse and Taylor. Your room is at the end of the row." She slid a key toward them. "Fifty bucks. Cash, check, or charge, doesn't matter to me."

"Two rooms," Taylor said.

The woman's eyebrows rose as she looked at the two. Jesse felt her take in their inebriated state, the bags of takeout, and then the woman laughed. "Sorry, girly. You're just going to have to make up with your stud muffin 'cause you got the last room I had."

"He's not my stud muffin," Taylor mumbled.

Jesse hoped he'd be able to get her to the room before she fell asleep. He slid the cash toward the motel clerk and smiled. "One room will be fine, thanks." He took the key and put his hand on Taylor's back, steering her out the door toward the overhang. The motel's rooms all opened up onto the parking lot, and Jesse found theirs at the end of the row. The Cowboy's Bunk looked like it had been built in the fifties and had never seen a remodel. It was so out of date that it'd now qualify as retro-modern.

He unlocked the door, worried what they'd find. When he flipped on the light, he was pleasantly surprised. The room was clean and smelled of lemon. He set the food sack on the small table in front of the window and unpacked their late-night snack.

Taylor fell into one of the chairs. "You won."

"You've already forgotten?" He sat across from her, unwrapping his burger.

She glared at him as she took a large bite, wiped her mouth, and responded. "Nope, just stating a fact. I worked that artist for years, and you walk in, and in one visit you convince him to use the gallery."

"What can I say, I'm good with people. It's all those years of interviews on the rodeo circuit. People are drawn to happy people." He dipped a fry into the special sauce provided. "These would be better with horseradish sauce."

"You're saying I'm not a happy person?" Taylor pointed her half-eaten burger at him.

"Sometimes, I think you aren't happy at all. Not at work, not in your own skin." He stroked the top of her hand holding the burger. "Why aren't you happy, Taylor? You've got it all."

A laugh erupted. "Seriously? What do I have?"

"A family who loves you. A great job. An amazing education. Friends. You look like a million bucks." Jesse shook his head. "What don't you have?"

Taylor polished off her hamburger before answering. "I live with my parents. The only person who ever noticed anything I did, my grandfather, died last year. I work too much and have no life outside the gallery and the events my folks insist I attend." She flipped her hair back. "The good looks are genetic. Not something I earned, or even worked at, so they don't count. Besides, there are a lot of pretty women. I want to be more than that."

"So you're not dating anyone?" Jesse pressed, his heart slowing a bit while he waited for an answer.

"That's what you take away from this entire discussion? I'm admitting to my failed life, and you focus on my dating schedule?" Taylor wadded up the wrapper and threw it into the bag. "Three points."

"Bag's too close—I'll give you two." Jesse smiled. "I don't think you have a failed life. Look at me."

"Three or four time bull riding champion? Now working on owning an art gallery along with what, one or two working ranches?" Taylor sipped on her drink. "Sounds like a complete failure to me."

"Look past the trappings. My brother is married to his high school sweetheart with three kids now. My manager just found her soulmate, even though she had to marry the guy twice to realize it." Jesse wadded his own wrappings up, leaned back, and shot. The paper landed gracefully inside the paper bag. "And I don't own a speck of land. The place I stay at in Boise is my brother's. Tell me, who's the loser?"

"Then get married. Have baby bull riders. There must be a lot of women out there wanting to play that role." Taylor rolled her eyes. "Like Amanda."

"I think our taxi driver has his heart set on little Miss Amanda. I wonder if she knows it yet." He chuckled. "But you're right; there are plenty of women who want to 'play' the part." He used air quotes to emphasize his words.

"You don't know who you'll fall in love with until you try."

He shook his head. "Now, I think you're wrong there. You can't try to be in love. Either it happens, or it doesn't. Believe me, I've tried out a lot of women."

"You sound like a man whore." She laughed.

"I probably was." He stared at her face, noticing the curve that he'd tried so hard to capture that day in class. No, he hadn't ever been in love. Not before. Now all he could do was think about her. Make excuses to be with her. Even now, sitting so close to her, a bed within arm's reach, all he wanted to do was reach out and touch her face. To let his fingers trace the curve that had eluded him as he tried to sketch her.

"Now you want true love?" she asked, her voice breathless.

"Would you believe me if I said yes?" Jesse touched her hand, one finger caressing the open palm.

"Tonight? I'd believe you if you told me you were Elvis reincarnated." She smiled and leaned forward, kissing him over the table, her lips so soft, but so needy. His head swam in images. Taylor laughing at the opening, her thoughtful gaze during the visit to the artist, the wind blowing through her hair on the drive here. Taylor. Something clicked in the back of his mind as if he'd been looking for her all his life. He pulled her closer, wanting more. The smell of cinnamon alcohol broke through the spell.

He gently pushed her aside. "You're drunk."

"True, but I know what I want. Let me just be Taylor. Just for tonight." She stood and held out her hand to him. "I promise I'll respect you in the morning."

And he went to her.

• • •

Sunlight streamed into the room through a crack in the cowboy-print curtains. Her head pounded. She rolled away from the light to face the bathroom, and realized she was alone in the bed. Taylor sat up, pulling the sheet around her. She took in the room that had seemed charming last night. In the bright morning light the décor just seemed walk-of-shame sad.

A bottle of water and a single-use pack of extra-strength OTC painkiller sat on the end table next to a note. She picked it up and read aloud to the empty room. "Take these. See you soon. Your ride will be here at nine. Jesse."

She shook her head, then winced at the pain. Unscrewing the cap, she took the painkillers and then downed the water. Stupid to get drunk with Jesse Sullivan. Stupid to open her heart. If she remembered correctly, she'd been the one to say, "Yes, let's have wild monkey sex." All after, he'd told her he was looking for more than just a good time. She was now a part of Jesse's harem.

She closed her eyes, remembering last night. How gentle he'd been. How his gaze had searched her face. She had vague memories of kissing and touching. Had they done anything more? She couldn't remember. Her clearest memory was of cuddling with Jesse while he mumbled words she couldn't quite remember into her ear. He kept repeating her name, over and over. Taylor, Taylor.

"Stop it." She forced her eyes open and glanced at the clock. 8:30. If his note was right, she'd be out of here in thirty minutes. She headed to the shower to wash away the memories of last night from her body, and hopefully, from her mind.

The knock on the door came right at nine. Dressed in last night's clothes, Taylor grabbed her purse and checked herself out in the mirror. No way around it, she looked like the poster child for the walk of shame. Grimacing, she opened the door.

Angie stood there, her big hair gleaming in the sunshine. For the love of God, was she wearing a leopard-print stretch jumpsuit with kitten heels? She jangled keys in front of her.

"Hey. You look … Well, let's just get you home so you can freshen up before you go into the gallery."

Taylor opened the door wider, letting Angie in. "How did you get here?" Glancing around the parking lot she saw only one car parked a few slots down.

"Jesse called me. He left early for Boise and didn't want to wake you. He's got to leave on time for the rodeo this weekend. If he misses another interview, Barb's going to wring his neck." She glanced at her watch. "He left about two hours ago. I've been having coffee with Maggie."

"He called you to come and get me?" Taylor didn't know if she was still a little woozy from last night, or if she'd just stepped into a weird Jesse-world where his mommy cleaned up his one-night stand mistakes. She figured the latter. They walked over to the car, and Taylor slid into the passenger seat.

"Look, I wasn't the best role model for my sons. And their dad, well, he kind of fell apart after I left. I feel bad about that. But neither Jesse nor James learned how to say the right things or deal with real feelings." Angie pulled out a compact and checked her ruby-red lipstick. Deciding she'd missed a spot, she reapplied another coat.

"So he asks his mom to clean up his messes," Taylor said. Angie gunned the engine and pulled out of the parking lot.

Angie put her lipstick back into her open purse and focused on Taylor. "Now that's where you're wrong. The fact that he left is a good thing."

"In what possible way could running out after a one-night stand be considered a good thing?" Taylor asked. Angie pulled the car up to a drive-through coffee shack. It was only large enough for two people to stand in and make coffee all day. Taylor found her wallet in her purse, pushing aside the signed contract. "I'm buying, you want something?"

"Large, black," Angie ordered and handed Taylor's twenty over to pay for their coffees. The window to the coffee shack closed. She added, "He would have stayed if he hadn't been scared out of his mind. And the only reason he'd be scared after a night with a beautiful woman?"

"How the hell would I know?" Taylor leaned her head back and closed her eyes. The coffee shack employee handed Angie the two cups, filling the small interior with the dark roast aroma. Angie angled the car back onto the street and took the entrance to the freeway headed toward Boise. The woman drove like she was on a NASCAR track. Taylor tugged on her seatbelt.

Once the car had merged into the light traffic, she glanced at Angie. "Fine, I give up, what would scare the Bull Rider Jesse Sullivan?"

"You have my youngest son on the ropes. Even Maggie saw it last night." Angie lightly tapped Taylor on the hand. "Jesse's in love."

Chapter 8

When Angie dropped Taylor off at the parking lot in back of the gallery, she quickly unlocked the car and headed to the house, hoping no one saw her walk of shame. At the DeMarco house, Taylor quietly snuck in, only to find her mom and dad had already left. It was after one in the afternoon by the time Taylor arrived at the gallery, way past her normal schedule.

Brit had opened and was working with a corporate customer when Taylor walked in. Taylor pointed to her office and disappeared behind the door as quickly as she could without breaking into a run. Angie had to be wrong. *I bet she says that to all of Jesse's girls.*

She stared at the computer as it booted up, willing her mind to get lost in the day-to-day gallery activities. Next week, they had a teacher from the nearby elementary school bringing a class in for a field trip. She'd have to have Brit do the tour and ask Angie to work earlier that day. She could just imagine the commentary Angie would provide for the kids.

She adjusted the work schedule, thankful Angie was scheduled late today. Maybe by the time she saw Jesse's mom again, Taylor would have already gotten the 'Dear Jane e-mail or text from Jesse. Then she wouldn't have to think about his mom's words.

She pulled the contract out of her purse and stuffed it into a file, pushing it aside on her desk. She should be ecstatic about bringing in a new talent to the gallery. She should be thinking about scheduling the show's opening, sending the contract over to the lawyers to get it finalized, and setting it up in the gallery's accounting system. She should be working.

She jumped when her phone rang. *Stupid*, she thought, and clicked the phone to answer.

"Taylor DeMarco." At first, she didn't think anyone was on the line, and she checked the display to see if she'd been disconnected. "Hello?"

"You got back." Jesse's voice rumbled through the phone and she thought of him whispering her name over and over in her ear last night.

She pressed her lips together, willing away the memory. "No thanks to you. Who dumps a date an hour away from home?"

He chuckled, and she squirmed at the sound. She should have pretended it didn't matter. Once again, he had the upper hand.

"Didn't you tell me it wasn't a date?" Before she could answer, he continued. "Sorry about that. I told Barb I'd be here for an early interview, so I had a plane to catch. And you looked so sweet, snoring your way through your dreams."

"I don't snore." Did she? She hadn't slept with anyone for years.

"Whatever you have to tell yourself, sweetheart. Anyway, what are you doing this weekend?" Jesse paused, then added, "Can you come to Wyoming?"

"Wyoming, vacation hot spot to the stars? Actually, I was just telling Brit how I wanted to spend a hot, dry weekend in Wyoming. Just me and the tumbleweeds." She bit her lip.

"Seriously, it's not that bad. And I'll make up for this morning by taking you out to dinner after the rodeo tonight." He paused. "I think we should talk. We're going to be working together and I'd hate for last night to, well, mess with our business relationship."

Taylor's heart sank. He was mending fences because of the gallery. "We could talk when you get back."

"I'd rather do it tonight before I lose my nerve." Jesse mumbled to someone on his end of the line. "Look, I've got to go. There will be a ticket waiting for you at the box office. Show starts at seven. I'll make reservations for dinner and a separate room at the hotel."

"I'll think about it." Taylor hesitated.

"Please come, Taylor," Jesse said, then paused. "Barb's fuming, I've got to go. Please come."

The line went dead.

She leaned back in her chair, tossing the phone on her desk. Brit caught the sliding cell before it dropped off the other side.

"Our new owner?" Brit set the phone down and slipped into one of the leather chairs in front of Taylor's desk. She adjusted the Anne Klein jacket that she wore over a silk tank and expensive jeans. Brit loved looking the part of an art curator, and her department store credit card statements proved it.

Brit absent-mindedly played with the fashionable chains hanging around her neck. Taylor narrowed her eyes as she watched her friend. "Why would you think that?"

Brit threw her head back and laughed. Finally, she looked at Taylor. "Seriously? I could see that guy had you twisted in knots since the night he showed up at the opening." Brit leaned forward. "So, you two doing the nasty?"

Taylor smiled in spite of herself. Brit could make her laugh at anything. "It's not any of your business."

Brit's eyes widened. "Oh. My. God. I was teasing, but you are so jumping his bones, aren't you?"

Heat ran to Taylor's face as she thought about the previous night. How gentle Jesse had been touching her, caressing her body, as if she were his piece of clay and he was molding her into a masterpiece.

"Earth to Taylor." Brit snapped her fingers. "Seriously, the boy is a player. You need to keep your heart protected this time. I don't want to be picking you up off the floor when he gets bored with playing fancy pants art dealer."

"I know. I don't know what he wants, or what I want, for that matter. And it was only once. So no talking about this." Taylor frowned, thinking about the call. "He wants me to meet him out of town this weekend so we can talk."

Brit pursed her lips. "Road booty call?"

"I don't think so. He seemed sincere." Taylor wondered if last night had surprised him as much as it had her. And if her memory was clear, she'd started the physical contact. She'd been the aggressor. He probably thought she was playing up to the new boss. The heat on her cheeks felt like fire now.

"You're going to go. Fly out and be his road toy."

Taylor started searching for a flight. "I'm not having sex with him. I'm getting this whole thing cleared up and past us, for the good of the gallery." She looked at her assistant. "You have Angie to help out this afternoon and all day Saturday, right?"

Brit shook her head. "Tomorrow, yes. But Angie just called. She's got an appointment or something today. This is the third one in the last week."

"From what I've learned, Angie has a habit of being a flake. Maybe I shouldn't go." Taylor leaned back in her chair, turning her attention from the computer to Brit.

"You think I can't handle the gallery by myself for," she glanced at her watch, "four hours? I used to open and close on your days off by myself. What, you think I've become needy in the last day or so??"

"It's not that I don't think you can deal," Taylor said. "Hell, I'm probably just trying to catch a lifeline here and talk myself out of going."

"Then don't go. You're a smart, intelligent woman. You don't need to be running off because Mr. Handsome Cowboy snaps his fingers."

Taylor laughed. "I'm not going because Jesse snapped his fingers. I need to know more about him, especially if I'm going to stop my folks from selling to him before I can get the funding package set. Mike says he just needs a few weeks."

A bell on the front door announced a new customer. Brit slipped out of her chair and went to greet the new arrival. Standing in the office door, she hesitated and waited until Taylor acknowledged her.

"What?"

Brit cocked her head and met Taylor's eyes. "Go ahead, play secret agent. Just remember what I told you. Keep your heart locked up. I worry about you."

Taylor watched her friend leave the office. Her fingers paused over the keyboard, wondering if this was totally stupid. Then she hit enter and picked up her purse. She had a plane to catch and she needed to pack an overnight bag.

She glanced at Marvin's contract. No use messing with it today. She'd get it over to Mike first thing on Monday. Besides, as it was Jesse's first contract, there were probably some legal things that they needed to set up.

• • •

Jesse paced in front of the arrival gate, waiting for her plane to land. Calling her had been stupid, impulsive, and ill-considered. Yet, he'd never been so sure of anything in his life. For years, he'd looked for the kind of love that James had with Lizzie. To love someone so much, well, he would give up anything to be with that person. He smiled as the thought came to him; he was more his mother's son than he would like to admit.

Inviting Taylor down to Casper without taking the time to think through what had happened had been impulsive. It's not like he hadn't had drunken sex before. Or even a one-night stand. But he'd never woken up early and watched the angel sleeping next to him breathe. His fingers had itched to pick up a pencil and draw the curve of her arm as it had draped over her chest, her hand curling up toward her face. He caught a glimpse of his reflection in the mirror. Man, he had it bad. An announcement came over the loud speaker that the Salt Lake flight had just landed. He felt bad for her having to fly to SLC then out to Casper, but the airlines liked to route their planes through regional hubs rather than send direct flights. Taylor's flight had taken four hours, but she almost could have driven the distance faster. Brit had been curt when he'd called the gallery to see what time Taylor's flight would be landing. Brit had been hesitant to give him the details, even after he'd explained he wanted to pick Taylor up since his interviews were over.

"I don't think this is a good idea," Brit wavered.

He wondered if she'd been talking about giving him the information or the whole idea of him and Taylor together. Had Taylor told her best friend about last night? He snorted. Of course she had. Women. They couldn't keep a secret to save their lives.

Then again, he hadn't kept their night together a secret, either. After all, he had told his mother. He had wanted some sort of approval, or at the very least, support that he wasn't jumping off a cliff. Of course, that was exactly what he was doing.

He glanced at the approaching crowd from the airplane. Would she see him if he took off and ran? He could hire her a driver, set her up in a hotel room, maybe even send Barb over to explain he was too busy to see her. He should be down at the barns checking out his tack and staring down the bulls. He briefly wondered which one he would be riding later that night. Lost in his escape plan, he didn't notice her until she put a hand on his arm.

"Jesse, what are you doing here?" Taylor looked up at him, confusion evident in her face.

He pushed aside his fears and leaned in to kiss her cheek. "I invited you down. What, you thought I'd just send a car? Or let you take a taxi? What kind of jerk does that?"

"I just didn't expect ..." Taylor trailed off.

Jesse reached for her carry-on bag slung over her shoulder, ignoring her pause. "You have checked baggage?"

When she shook her head, he was surprised. Taylor didn't seem like the kind of girl who only traveled with one bag, even for a short weekend getaway. He'd expected two, maybe even three more bags. *See, you don't know her at all.* He brushed away the thought. They had time to learn about each other. As long as she felt the same way, there would be plenty of time.

He put his hand on the small of her back and maneuvered her toward the exit. "Let's get you set up at the hotel; then, I'll take you to the barn and introduce you to the bulls who want to crush me tonight."

Taylor laughed. "Sounds like fun. Is one of them named Amanda?"

"Jeez, you're never going to let me live that one down, are you? I swear," Jesse held up a hand in a three-finger Boy Scout salute, "there was never anything between Amanda and me. I was nice to her because she is Maggie's daughter."

They stepped out into the bright Wyoming sunshine. "I believe you, I'm just not sure Amanda does."

He let that comment slide. Driving through the edge of town, the two remained quiet in the rental car Jesse had picked up when he arrived that morning. He typically rented, even if the car stayed parked at the hotel the entire weekend. He liked having options.

They reached the hotel about twenty minutes later. Jesse waited in the lobby while Taylor ran up to the room to drop off her bag and freshen up. He watched the elevator door close behind her, kicking himself for not escorting her. *Slow down,* he thought. *You don't even know if she likes you.* At least she'd confirmed last night that she wasn't dating anyone. He thought about her kiss last night, and slid down into one of the lobby couches.

"Jesse Sullivan," a man's voice boomed. Jesse turned and looked into Hunter Martin's face. "Shouldn't you be hanging around the rodeo grounds looking for tonight's after-show party girl?"

Jesse stood, shaking Hunter's hand. He liked the guy. Barb had done well for herself. "I figured you'd be staying back in Boise this weekend. Doesn't Kadi have a competition?"

The men sank down into the couches, Hunter taking the couch that mirrored the one Jesse was sitting in. "When doesn't Kadi have a competition? I swear that niece of mine is horse crazy. My dad's doing cheerleading duty this weekend. Barb and I decided to take a weekend for ourselves."

"Mixing business with pleasure."

"Summer keeps Barb busy, so I have to grab her time when I can." Hunter smiled. "She loves her job. Although, I don't get why, having to corral the likes of you all the time."

"Well, soon I won't be the one she's chasing around." Jesse slung his arm over the top of the couch.

Hunter leaned forward. "I hear; congrats. If you need a good accountant or lawyer, let me know. I can give Barb a few names of people that worked with the dairy before we got so big we hired a full-time staff."

Jesse groaned. "I'm pretty sure I'll need referrals. I know Barb's having George look over the contract, but I don't think he wants to be involved in all the day-to-day stuff. I'd rather not use the current gallery lawyer. I'd just feel better knowing I hired the guy and he has my back, you know?"

"Smart man." Hunter grinned. "Next time I see you, you'll probably be stuffed into a suit with a Bluetooth stuck in your ear. Jesse Sullivan, art dealer."

"Now, don't go crazy on me. I'm pretty sure art dealers don't wear the monkey suit. Aren't we supposed to dress like creative types?" Jesse thought about the one, lone suit hanging in his closet back home.

"I think those are the artists, not the gallery owners." Hunter stood and greeted his wife as Barb joined them.

"I didn't think I'd see the two of you chatting it up." Barb kissed Hunter and then turned her attention to Jesse. "Don't you have bull rider duties to perform?"

"Just waiting for Taylor, then I'll go down and play the role," Jesse drawled.

Barb, who had been drawing circles on her husband's leg with her French-tipped fingernail, stopped and frowned. "Taylor's here?"

"Don't look like that. I invited her."

Barb leaned forward. "I don't think that's the best idea you've ever had."

Hunter put his hand on Barb's back. Jesse saw the movement. Was he supporting her? Or warning her?

"Look, I'm not known for great ideas. But I think this girl may be the one."

Barb's eyes widened. "Jesse, slow down. You need to think about this. Taylor is your gallery manager. Having fun is one thing, but when you have to see that person daily, well, relationships like that can get complicated."

"I'm not a kid, Barb." Jesse's words came out harsher than he'd wanted. "I like the girl. Maybe more. But I'm not an idiot. If she's not interested she'll tell me, and we can go back to whatever friendly relationship we had before. I need to know where I stand."

"I think you're treading on thin ice, here," Barb warned.

"Now that doesn't sound like the Jesse I'm beginning to know at all."

Jesse turned his head to see Taylor standing in front of them. He took in the sight of her. Skintight stretch jeans, a silk tank in brilliant blue, her hair loose around her shoulders. He stopped at her feet and grinned—she had on cowboy boots. He was in love.

Barb stood and Hunter followed her lead. "Taylor, so nice to see you." She made the introductions between Hunter and Taylor.

"We were about to grab some dinner before the event. Do you two want to join us?"

Jesse shook his head. "You know I can't eat before I ride." He grinned at Taylor. "I swear the bulls can smell a cheeseburger or a T-bone steak on your breath. Riders get killed that way."

"So most riders are vegetarians? At least on days they compete?" Taylor sat down on the sofa next to Jesse. "That's fascinating, I've never heard that before."

"Because it's just Jesse's theory, not reality." Barb laughed. "Believe me, the more you hang around the guy, the easier it will be to figure out his bullcrap."

"Ouch, that's harsh." Jesse pretended to be shot to the stomach.

"I have to be honest with you, it's in our contract." Barb gave him a sweet smile, which didn't fool him in the least.

"Hunter, you should have run when you had the chance." Jesse glanced over at Barb's husband, who was listening to the verbal bantering like it was Wimbledon, each insult another ball over the net.

The man held up his hands in mock surrender. "Don't get me in the middle of this. Taylor, sometimes the most prudent path is the one where you step aside and let the children play through."

Jesse watched as Taylor bit back a smile. The girl would hold her own with the Shawnee group, that was for sure. He focused on her. "Do you want to go eat with Barb and Hunter?"

Taylor frowned. "I thought you were taking me to the barn?"

"I can. But if you'd rather grab some food?" He knew they were being polite with each other. After last night he didn't want to push the girl. They needed some time alone to talk.

Taylor glanced at Barb. "Thanks for the offer, but we've got some things to talk about." Taylor flushed red. "About the gallery, I mean."

Barb and Hunter exchanged a look Jesse couldn't read. That was the thing about couples, they all had their own secret looks. Moments where they knew what the other person was saying without using a single word. He'd like that kind of relationship someday. "Taylor flew down to hammer some things out about the sale, so I guess we shouldn't waste her time."

"Invitation's always open. Maybe the four of us can get together for breakfast tomorrow before Hunter and I fly home." Barb stood and pulled Hunter to his feet. "Take me and feed me."

"See what happens when you're old married folk? The food is more important than time together," Hunter whispered loudly to Taylor.

Barb slapped his arm. "Don't you even go there, mister. You and I were married folk before we even started dating." When she saw Taylor's shocked face she laughed. "Long story. I'll set up a girl's night with Angie and Lizzie when we get home and catch you up on all the Shawnee gossip you're going to need if you're dating Jesse."

Taylor protested, "We're not dating."

Barb and Hunter strolled away from the couches. "Whatever you have to tell yourself."

Jesse took Taylor's hand. "Barb's not known for her tact. Probably because she's my manager, she's learned to say what's on her mind. Right now, she thinks we're going down the wrong path. That someone's going to get hurt."

He saw Taylor's shoulders tighten. She sighed and leaned back into the cushions. "Brit's saying the same thing. What is this, Jesse? A drunken mistake?"

"I don't think so." Jesse turned and watched her. "I need to know if you feel anything for me. I know it's early and we barely know each other. But I have to tell you, I want this to work."

"So you don't think this will ruin us working together?" Taylor's gaze found his, her look was guarded.

"I don't know. I just know I want to try. Me. You. Us." Jesse leaned in to kiss her, but his phone rang. "Horrible timing." He pulled the phone off its holster on his belt and glared at the display. "The rodeo commissioner. I need to take this."

Chapter 9

Jesse walked away, and Taylor thought about what he'd said. She's been expecting a sorry-about-last-night-can-we-just-forget-it-ever-happened speech. Instead, she thought she'd just been asked to go steady. The man was impossible to read. He made her want to stand and do her hoppy version of a victory dance. She glanced around the elegant lobby. Probably not the place.

Jesse returned and pulled her off the couch. "Come on. They need me down at the barn. More publicity pictures that Barb forgot to tell me about. I'm meeting the mayor and his daughter, the reigning rodeo queen, for promotional stuff."

"I could just stay here and catch up with Barb and Hunter." Taylor glanced around the empty lobby, wondering where the couple had disappeared to.

"Believe me, we'll have time to talk." Jesse took her arm and they walked out of the marble lobby to the parking lot. The hotel could have been smack-dab in the middle of downtown Boise except for all the pickups and horse trailers in the parking lot.

She watched the town pass by as Jesse followed the car's GPS toward the rodeo grounds. Franchise fast food was taking over the world. Of the last five drive-in eateries they'd passed, each one of them was available in or near Boise. The homogenization of America, one meal at a time. Taylor noticed that, even in an unfamiliar city, Jesse looked cool and in control. He had one hand on the wheel, leaning toward the open window. She would have been a mess, wondering if she'd missed a turn, or worse, couldn't get to the correct side of the road to turn onto her exit. He seemed to know exactly where he was and where he needed to go. No different here than in his own stomping ground. Taylor wondered if that was just his style, a rolling stone, comfortable anywhere.

She relaxed and decided to let the day go where it went. When she opened her mouth to ask about traveling on the road, instead, she said, "I can't believe you left me this morning."

Jesse's face turned red but he didn't meet her eyes. "I'm an idiot, what can I say?"

"Sorry?" Taylor hadn't wanted to talk about this until after he rode. If he was too upset and couldn't focus the bull could kill him. She shook the thought away; as far as she could see, Jesse Sullivan didn't get upset over anything. The man was an ice cube. Well, except for last night. She worried her own face was turning colors as she remembered their night together.

"I am sorry. I never meant for us to stay over in Ontario. I never meant for our night to go so long." He glanced at her this time. "Of course, you're partially to blame for that."

"Me?" Taylor knew her face was red now. He blamed her?

Jesse turned off the main road and Taylor could see the outdoor grandstand sitting behind a large parking lot. "You wouldn't lose. If I'd known you were that good at darts I would have demanded we play shuffleboard."

"I played a bit in college," Taylor admitted. "But you did win. If I remember right."

"After we played all night." Jesse pulled the car into a parking spot near the barns. He turned off the car and looked at her. "Actually, I expected to beat you in three straight games. I underestimated you. I won't do that again."

She watched him leave the car, wondering if he was already underestimating her. She pushed the thought away and climbed out of the car, hurrying to catch up. Time to find out what made this guy tick. He could say all the pretty words he wanted, but when it all shook out, they were on opposite sides of the deal. She had to protect her interest in the gallery at all costs. She put on her sales smile and called out to him, "Hold up."

For the next two hours Jesse showed her the life of a rodeo star. He did a couple of interviews, meeting and greeting like he was a politician running for office. Then he took her to the barn where they kept the livestock. The strong smell of bull hit her nostrils. The animals were hot in the closed-in area. Fans blew air around the pens, trying to keep them cool.

She walked up to a gate, and the bull in the pen eyed her with an intense glare. "It's like he sees me as the enemy."

Jesse pulled her back a few steps. "He probably does. Bulls are smart. I swear there are a few that I hadn't rode in years that still remember me just by the sound of my voice. When I'd watched their ride videos, they'd twisted right on leaving the gate with every rider. But for me, they'd twist left. Like they knew I'd figured out their pattern and had to switch it up."

"You're kidding me." Taylor glanced up into Jesse's face, looking for a trace of a smile to give his prank away.

Jesse held his hand up in a vow symbol. "I swear on my mama's grave." Then he smiled. "I guess that saying doesn't work anymore, now that we know Angie is alive."

Taylor put her hand on his forearm. "That must have been hard. When she left, I mean."

Jesse didn't say anything, but led her over to a straw bale where they sat together. Jesse leaned forward and put his forearms on his thighs. "I didn't understand for a long time. James was mad at her. I just missed her. So I became the funny kid. The kid everyone wanted around, the boy every girl wanted. I thought, maybe if I was good enough, she'd come back."

"Hard for a little kid to carry that around."

"Cry me a river. Man, I've never admitted that to anyone before. I must look like a loser." Jesse didn't look at her.

An announcement came over the loudspeaker calling the riders to the gate.

He stood and hurried her out of the barn. Handing her a ticket, he pushed her through a door leading to the grandstands. "You'll be sitting with Barb and Hunter. I'll come find you afterward."

She turned back to say good luck, but the door had already shut behind him. *Just a little boy looking for love.* Taylor felt horrible. She understood now what her betrayal and knew what the loss of the gallery would do to Jesse. But better him than her. Pain hit her gut. She liked Jesse. Hell, if the gallery weren't in play, she'd throw caution to the wind and see where the relationship went. At least it would be fun. But she couldn't let him in, not now. She shouldn't have come to Wyoming. *Just get through the day.* She kept the mantra going until she reached her seat. Barb handed her a corn dog and a packet of mustard.

"We thought you might need a snack." Barb scooted over toward Hunter, giving Taylor room to sit down and get settled.

"Thanks." Taylor glanced around. "Anywhere I'd be able to get a beer?"

Hunter stood. "I'll run. Barb?"

"Soda. Not diet. I hate the taste," Barb admitted to Taylor.

"You don't have to go; I can get my own drink," Taylor protested.

"Let him go. It's an excuse for him to get a second drink. He loves it when I'm playing designated driver." Barb slapped her husband on the butt as he stepped past her.

Taylor swirled the mustard from the packet onto the still-hot corn dog. The smell of the mustard bit her senses. They must have arrived just before she had. She bit into the cornmeal-covered hot dog and groaned in pleasure. Fried heaven. In August, she'd made daily trips to the state fairgrounds for lunch to delight in the summer treat.

"Lizzie loves her corn dogs, too. Especially when she's pregnant." Barb's lips curled into a smile. "You got something to tell us?"

Taylor wiped mustard off her mouth with a napkin. "Yeah, I love corn dogs."

"You're bad," Barb said, teasing her. "Jesse's been a friend for a long time. He's kind of like a little brother. I'd hate to see his heart get broken."

Taylor finished the corn dog before she answered. Fear clutched at her as she thought about what might have happened last night. Had she already gone too far to turn back? Had that been why he'd called? A second taste of Taylor? She pushed the thought away. "For Mr. Sullivan being such a player—and don't deny it, I've heard the rumors—you sure make him sound like a softie."

"I've seen him with a lot of girls; I won't deny that. But he's never looked at any of them the way he looks at you. I've been part of that family for years, even when we were kids. Jesse, his brother, and Lizzie, well, the four of us were tight. We'd be at my house or Lizzie's if we weren't hanging out at the river." Barb glanced through the crowd, apparently searching for someone. "I hate to be the one who tells you, but he cares about you."

Taylor took in the large arena, feeling the excitement of the crowd and families sitting around her. She wondered, could this be her life? Watching Jesse risk his neck just to prove he could stay on a bull for eight seconds? "I don't think so." She dug in her purse, avoiding Barb's scrutiny. "We're too different. I mean, Jesse's amazing, but his life is exciting and interesting. I'm pretty boring if you get to know me. I'm sure he's just being nice."

She felt Barb's hand on her arm and gave up the fake searching. "Believe me, Jesse cares for you. And if you're just playing him, please stop."

Taylor couldn't hear anything else. The crowd noise disappeared, and all she could think about was kissing him last night. The more she thought about it, the more convinced she was that they hadn't made love. Hell, she'd done more in Ken's back seat when she was trying to stay a virgin in high school. Yet, for some reason, this felt more intimate.

Finally, she looked at Barb. "I don't want to hurt him."

"I guess I'll have to take that for my answer, then." Barb glanced up at Hunter who'd returned with the drinks. She smiled and her voice softened. "Hey, baby."

Hunter stared at the women as he handed over the beer to Taylor. Barb took the soda and ice cream sandwich. "Should I leave and come back later?"

Taylor quickly said, "We're done. Girl talk, you know."

Hunter slipped into his seat next to his wife, shooting her an I-told-you-to-stay-out-of-it look. Barb responded with a wide-eyed innocent shrug as she unwrapped the ice cream.

"How'd you know I was craving this?" She leaned her head against Hunter's arm and took a bite.

Taylor watched as Hunter brushed a wild curl that had escaped Barb's hair clip, his face filled with so much love and tenderness it made Taylor look away. She felt as though she was intruding on their intimacy. Someday, she'd have a love like that. Jesse's face filled her mind. She couldn't forget the way he had whispered her name.

Her soul mate, the love of her life, was not going to be Jesse Sullivan, bull rider. No way. She wanted someone stable, secure, and, yes, boring. Boring would be good. As she tried convincing herself that she wouldn't fall for Jesse's lines, the announcer called up the first contestant.

Barb nudged her. "That's Carl. He's one of my riders. He's almost as good as Jesse."

Hunter laughed. "Not one of your other guys is in Jesse's league. When he retires you're going to have to find a new star for your male harem."

"They are not my harem. I'm just their manager." Barb slapped Hunter's arm playfully.

"Not to mention, you're their best friend, their bail bondsman, their mother, and their accountant," Hunter responded, his voice playful.

The crowd quieted and leaned forward to watch the gate release. Taylor focused on the gate, watching the cowboy sitting on the bull. Only his shoulders and hat showed through the bars. She flinched as she saw the bull react to the rider's weight. Carl pulled back, waiting for the animal to calm. Finally, the bull and rider were settled. The man in the chute pushed his hat further down on his head, lifted his free arm, and nodded his readiness to the gate handler.

The gate flew open, and the bull came out of the chute bucking and twisting. Taylor thought of Jesse's comment about the bull being able to read its rider as she watched the dance between the massive animal and Barb's client. She held her breath as the seconds counted down. Finally, the buzzer announced the eight seconds had passed. Barb stood and cheered. Taylor watched as a rider on a horse came near the bull. The bull rider threw himself off the large animal and onto the back of the horse.

"Not the most graceful dismount," Hunter said, chuckling.

"Doesn't matter. The judging is done." Barb giggled and clapped louder. "Great job, Carl!" She sat back down on the bench to await the score. "Your Jesse may have some competition tonight. I swear that kid gets better every time he rides. And Old Hickory is a great bull; he's got a high buck-off percentage, so that will increase Carl's score." Barb wiggled in her seat. "I'm so happy for him. If he wins, I'll have to call all his sponsors and up his appearance price."

"My girl, always the optimist." Hunter shook his head.

"What? He deserves to be compensated for a good ride. Hell, that was a great ride. He keeps that up, and I'll have two riders in the Vegas finals in December." Barb looked over at Taylor. "You'll learn the lingo soon enough."

"He's not my Jesse ..." Taylor started to say, but Barb shushed her when the announcers started talking again. Eventually, they announced his score. Eighty-seven.

Barb sighed. "It's good, but it should have been better. Sometimes, the judges are a little tight early in the night. I hope it holds."

Taylor watched the next few riders, and no one stayed on for the full eight seconds. So far, Carl was still in the lead. The loudspeaker announced Jesse Sullivan's name and Taylor's heart sank. She leaned forward, unable to breathe. She saw the black hat that Jesse had slipped on when he got out of the car. It was the final piece of his uniform to play the part of professional bull rider. No wonder he wanted to paint and focus on art. At least in a gallery, his chance of getting stomped on by a rampaging bull after being thrown off was slim to none. Although, art critics could be destructive to a new artist's career and mental well-being.

Jesse nodded his head and the gate flew open. Barb had told Taylor that his bull, Taste the Earth, hadn't ever been ridden for the full eight seconds. If Jesse could just stay on ... She watched the bull buck, and Jesse leaned so far back that his head nearly touched the bull's flanks. His free arm balanced his body against the bull's motion. Almost as fast, the bull regained his footing and twisted left, then right, trying to unseat his rider. Jesse stayed on. Taylor wanted to glance at the clock, but she couldn't stop watching.

The buzzer went off and Jesse let go, flying off the side of the bull. Before the animal could register he was gone, Jesse hopped on the corral fence and glanced through the grandstands. He caught her eye and grinned, waving his hat.

"Leave it to Jesse," Barb mumbled.

"He stayed on the bull—that's what he's supposed to do, right?" Taylor asked.

Barb sighed. "I was just hoping Carl might win this one. The kid's been in Jesse's shadow so long that he's beginning to grow mushrooms on his feet."

"He'll have his day. Jesse's retiring soon." Hunter smiled at Taylor. "He's becoming a fancy art dealer. You think you can tame the guy enough so he doesn't spit tobacco in your pretty shop?"

Taylor's eyes widened. "He chews?"

Barb slapped Hunter's leg. "He's just kidding you. Jesse doesn't smoke, chew or, as far as I know, do anything illegal. He does like his tequila, though."

"Yeah, I found that out," Taylor said, grinning. She wanted to add that he hadn't yet bought the art gallery. But like any good poker player, Taylor held on to her card. It would either be a wild card in the game, or just a joker. She didn't know if she could pull it off, or if her folks would even let her buy the gallery.

She cheered along with the crowd at Jesse's ninety-three score. The trio watched the rest of the riders, but even Taylor knew Jesse had clinched the win. She finished her beer just as Jesse slipped onto the bench next to her.

"Did you watch, or hide your eyes behind your hands?" Jesse handed long necks down the row. Barb waved hers off. Jesse cocked his head, examining her face. She flushed under his scrutiny. "Fine, don't tell me. It just means more beer for me."

Taylor took the offered bottle, cold and icy in her hand. "I watched. You're pretty good."

Jesse held a hand to his heart. "Faint praise. I'll die if you don't tell me how amazingly awesome I was tonight."

"Does it say rodeo groupie on my forehead?" Taylor asked.

Hunter laughed. "Get him, Taylor."

Barb leaned against her husband and watched Taylor and Jesse. "You two fight like an old married couple."

Jesse shook his head. "This isn't fighting, Barb; it's the courting ritual. She's into me."

Chapter 10

After they left Barb and Hunter at the rodeo, Jesse and Taylor drove across town to find dinner. Taylor groaned when he pulled the car into a steakhouse parking lot. "Sorry, I know we had steak last night, but the food's great. There are just not a lot of choices out here. This place does a mean mahi-mahi fish taco if you want something different."

"It's fine." Taylor got out of the car and waited for Jesse on the sidewalk. "You forgot your hat."

He took her arm and led her into the restaurant. "I'm off duty, so it stays in the car."

"Jesse, hold on a second." Taylor paused at the door. She searched his face, looking for an answer without asking the question. "Is this a date?"

His face didn't change, no flicker of amusement or horror. His grip tightened a little on her arm. "Do you want it to be?"

She hesitated, her brain shouting no. But something else shouted yes. The question was whether it came from her heart, or her body. Did it matter?

"Relax; I didn't ask you down here for a quickie. I think we need to talk about us." Jesse waited.

She nodded. "Okay, then." She walked through the door, feeling his presence so close behind her, and stopped in front of the hostess station.

The hostess led them to a secluded table near the window. "Our soup tonight is clam chowder. Our special is stuffed pork chop." She sat the menus on the table and left.

"My flight leaves tomorrow at noon." Taylor studied the menu.

"I'm heading out around the same time. Barb has me scheduled for interviews first thing in the morning, so no getting me drunk and taking advantage of me."

Her head shot up. Jesse wasn't looking at her, his head bent, studying the menu. She looked around the room and lowered her voice. "I didn't get you drunk."

"If that's your story," he said, looking up and grinning at her. The waitress arrived with water and took their drink order.

"Iced tea with lemon," Taylor announced. The two beers at the rodeo had already loosened her tongue too much. Soon, she'd be telling Jesse about her childhood and the numerous summer camps she'd attended. And how she was plotting with Mike to keep him from buying the gallery.

"Root beer for me."

They gave the waitress their food order as well. When she left, the table fell quiet.

Taylor set down the knife she'd been playing with. "Root beer?"

He shrugged. "I like it. What can I say? I'm a simple kind of guy."

She studied the man sitting in front of her. "So, you got me here; what did you want to say?"

The direct approach surprised him, she could tell. But he pulled himself up, squared his shoulders, and started. "I like you, Taylor. I mean, you're smart, funny, absolutely gorgeous, and I like spending time with you. You're the first thing I think of when I get up and the last thing I think of before I go to sleep." He paused and a sheepish smile crossed his face. "Not in a dirty way. Well, maybe a little."

She slapped his arm. "Jesse, you were winning points until that last bit. You need to learn when to shut up."

"Barb tells me that all the time." He grabbed a roll and tossed it to her. "Eat, you're grumpy."

"I'm not grumpy," Taylor said. She cut open the crusty warm bread and slathered butter on the inside. She took a bite, and watched as Jesse did the same with his roll. She thought about her conversation with Barb earlier. "You and Barb are close?"

"Yeah, but not in that way, if you're wondering. I had a huge crush on her when we were in high school, but she was older, and she and Lizzie, that's my brother's wife, were friends." He finished the rest of the roll in one bite. "She always saw me as James's little brother—even years later. Someone burned her badly, so for years, I don't think she even dated."

"Then she met Hunter, and he swept her off her feet?" Taylor asked.

"Kind of. She and Hunter have an interesting story. You'll have to ask her to tell you someday."

Taylor lifted her eyebrows. "You could tell me."

"Barb and Hunter were married before they fell in love. Kind of by accident." He shook his head. "Anyway, not my story to tell. Just wanted you to know that there wasn't ever anything going on between me and Barbie."

Taylor thought about Jesse's declaration. When the waitress brought their dinners, a T-bone for Jesse, salmon for her, she took a bite and then set her knife and fork down next to her plate.

"Uh oh, this can't be good." Jesse eyed his steak, then matched her movements and set his own flatware on the table. "Tell me what you're thinking."

"You think we should date?" She knew she was being blunt, and maybe obtuse, but the more direct she was, the better answers she got. Good or bad.

Jesse nodded his head and his lips curled into a grin. "Yep. I think we should date. Like tonight. Dinner, maybe a walk by the river, maybe a kiss."

"There's a river here?"

"You're missing the point. And I was making that part up, so I don't really know if there's a river. I would like to court you, Miss DeMarco." He reached over and took her hand. "What do you think? Are you even remotely interested?"

She felt like laughing, crying, or screaming, "Yes!" But Mike's face kept popping into her mind. And visions of the gallery. Her gallery. She wanted to be the owner, not just another manager, easily replaced. But that was tomorrow's worry. Tonight, a handsome man was interested in her. And she would enjoy the ride until it came to a screeching halt.

"I am interested, Mr. Sullivan, provided we take it slow, one day at a time."

"You make me sound like an addiction." Jesse picked up his knife and fork, slicing into the meat. He stabbed a piece onto his fork and showed her the gentle pink inside. "Perfect; medium rare."

She took a bite of her own dinner and wondered about her choice of words. Being near the man made her feel higher than any alcohol. The feeling was more intense than the time she had her appendix taken out and they'd sent her home with hydrocodone for the pain. Eventually, she'd stopped taking the pills. They'd invaded her dreams, making her run from nightmare monsters and painful emotions. Yes, being around Jesse Sullivan felt like a drug. And if she wasn't careful, she'd be homeless and out of work, like many of the addicted.

• • •

Jesse loved watching Taylor. The way she ate. The way she walked. And most important, the way she gave in to emotion when she laughed, her head thrown back, and her entire body a part of the experience.

He hadn't known exactly what to say when he had invited her to fly out for the rodeo. He just knew that there were too many miles between them, and he felt the distance like a concrete wall blocking their progress.

With dinner finished, he drove them back to the hotel. His room was on the same floor as Taylor's, so he walked her to her door. She swiped her card into the mechanical lock multiple times, with no luck. Stepping closer, he took the card from her. Putting two fingers on her chin, he pulled up her head and brushed the hair out of her face. He dropped his head down to meet hers and kissed her. His body reacted to the possibilities of the slow, soft kiss. He pulled away, finding her as breathless as he felt.

"Let me get that door," he said, his voice husky, betraying his desire. He swiped the card again, and this time the light turned from amber to a bright green. He opened the door for her and handed her the key.

"Come in." She took a step in, hesitating. "If you want to."

Jesse stood there and looked at her body. "You haven't heard a damn thing I've said all night, have you?"

"Of course I have."

He followed her into the room and watched as she tried to pull her boots off. He walked over and kneeled in front of her. He slowly pulled off one boot, then the other, his hand tracing imaginary lines down the inside of her calves. "I don't think so."

"What? What are you getting at?" Her voice sounded slightly tense. He smiled and looked up at her.

"I want to be here. To be with you. Why is that so hard to understand?" He sat next to her on the king size bed.

"I'm needy, what can I say?" Taylor laughed off Jesse's question.

"I doubt it." He took her hand, kissing the palm. The heat of her body next to his made him shiver. "You are amazing, successful, and beautiful. I don't think you need anything. I just have to make you want me."

"Hold up, cowboy." Taylor stood and walked away from the bed. Leaning against the dresser, she crossed her arms. "What happened last night?"

Jesse leaned back on the bed. "You're kidding, right?"

Her face flushed. "Stop playing games. Did we sleep together, or not?"

Jesse held out his hands. "Come here."

Taylor looked at him like he was holding a live snake. "Jesse …"

He interrupted her, "Just come closer."

Hesitantly, she walked to him, and he took both of her hands in his. He stood to meet her. "We did sleep together last night." He saw her cringe, but pushed on anyway. "Only sleep. I didn't want our first time to be alcohol induced. I want you to want me, not just drunken sex."

The relief on her face almost made him laugh, but a part of him wondered why it would have been so awful for her. He released one of her hands and caressed her cheek with his fingers.

"I didn't remember," she admitted to him. "If you haven't guessed by now, I'm a control freak and it scared me that I didn't remember."

"And that's why you came today." Jesse tucked a wayward strand of her blond hair behind her ear.

"One reason." She searched his face. "I don't know where this is going."

"Do we have to know tonight?" He tipped his head and let his lips gently touch the curve of her neck. He felt her shiver.

"One day at a time?" she asked breathlessly.

He spun her around, and they fell on the bed. "One moment at a time."

Their gazes locked, and when she nodded, he kissed her. Hard and demanding this time. Her lips were like diving into a shimmering pool on a hot summer day. Pulling back, he ran his hand down the curve of her cheek. The curve he couldn't seem to get right, even after drawing it over and over. He felt his body tighten as he looked at her. Right then, he knew if all he had was this one time, it would all be worth it.

He felt her hands unbuttoning his shirt as he focused on her neck, drinking in the smell of her—clean, floral, and all Taylor. He'd know if she was in a crowded room just by the traces of her scent that followed her as she moved. He moved his hand to her shirt; the neckline falling open, making room for his fingers to slip inside, feeling the lace of her bra. Soft pillows of flesh greeted his hand, and he groaned, his mouth still on her neck, vibrating the skin under his lips.

Abandoning the curve of her neck, his attention moved down her body to her breasts. Instead of lingering, he sat up and finished unbuttoning his own shirt. Taylor had pushed the front open, allowing the fabric to bunch up on his arms. He pulled off her tank. He pushed down the cups of her bra, revealing her pink and creamy breasts. Her nipples were hard and he took one in his mouth, lightly pinching the other between his fingertips. He felt her body rise to meet him, and he increased his pace, switching his attention from one breast to the other until she cried out.

He repositioned himself on the bed and unzipped her jeans, pulling the fabric over her narrow hips. The motion exposed a tiny, silk bikini that matched her black lacy bra. He smiled. Jennifer, his former girlfriend, had once called it sex underwear. Every time he'd seen Taylor in a state of undress, she always wore these silky delights. He abandoned all thought except stripping off the tiny lace and seeing what was hidden underneath.

He reached down and pulled off the small piece of fabric. Parting her legs, he leaned into her, licking her thighs all the way up to her hot core. He heard her short intake of breath as his mouth covered her, and he started exploring her with his tongue. As his warm breath hit her, she tightened until he slipped a finger into her moist opening. He felt her body arch into his mouth as she cried out.

Moving his tongue and finger in the same motion, he could feel her hands in his hair, urging him on. Suddenly, she pressed herself hard against his mouth, begging him to go faster. Listening to her cries of pleasure, Jesse felt his cock tighten against his jeans. She closed her thighs, pushing his head away from her, and sat up, pulling him toward her.

"My turn." She pushed him up off the bed and quickly unbuckled his jeans. He almost came with her touch, but pulled himself back. He wondered how long he'd be able to hold off if she was really doing what he imagined.

Her lips curved around the head of his penis and slipped down the shaft. He shifted, trying to think about anything other than her mouth on him, wanting to make it last longer than the eight seconds bull riders were teased about. Jesse needed this feeling to go on forever. She tugged and licked and teased until it was all he could do to not go over the edge. He put his hand on her shoulder, forcing out the words, "If you don't stop, I'll explode."

She pulled away and looked up at him. "Isn't that the point?" Her head dropped back down, and Jesse gave in.

When he finished, he stepped out of his jeans and crawled into bed next to her. He drew her back into his body and spooned her. "We're not done," he warned, whispering in her ear.

"I'm counting on it," she murmured back. He could tell she was almost asleep from the tone of her voice.

When Jesse awoke later, it was still dark, and he felt Taylor's legs pressing in against his hips. She'd climbed on top of him. He reached for her, pulling her down into a kiss. And they made love.

Chapter 11

This time, Taylor was the one to slip out of the bed, grab her clothes and her suitcase, and practically run to the elevator. She finally took a breath when the doors closed without Jesse's hand slipping in and preventing her escape.

She wasn't proud of her actions. When she'd woken up to feel his arm draped around her, she'd had to run. The echoes of him whispering her name in her ear as they fell back asleep after round two had haunted her thoughts. She'd had to get away. Before she'd let her heart speak and say stupid stuff. Like, "I love you, Jesse." Or, "Stay with me." He didn't want forever, not with her. No matter what he said, or what Barb claimed. One moment at a time had been enough. He'd agreed to her statement. And now, she felt like the fool. The very unprotected fool. Why hadn't she left him in the hallway? And why, oh, God, why, hadn't she insisted on a condom? This was not the way Taylor DeMarco acted. Ever.

A taxi sat outside the hotel, and she slid into the back. "Airport."

"No problem. What airline?" The taxi driver, a young woman with her hair cut short, asked as she started the engine, glancing in the mirror.

"United." Taylor didn't want to meet the girl's eyes. She didn't want any human contact to break her misery. She just wanted to leave and forget about last night's pleasure. The feel of his chest as she ran her hands across that tan, muscular body. The feel of his mouth against hers. The feel of his mouth on her neck, her breasts, her …

"You here for the rodeo?" The driver's voice broke into Taylor's memory, and she swallowed before answering.

"Seeing a friend," she said. Which was true, and not true at the same time. When Jesse arrived back in town she would simply explain that gallery business had called her back. As the soon-to-be new owner, he should understand. After that, she'd just have to keep from being alone with him. Ever again. She couldn't be one of Jesse's girls. Not a stop on the rodeo trail. She had responsibilities. She had the gallery. Or at least she hoped she had the gallery still.

Taylor pulled out her BlackBerry and thumbed through her e-mails. When she found one from Brit, she opened and read the short message.

Reading the words aloud, she frowned as the implication sunk in. "Found the contract on your desk. Dropped it off at Mike's, so one less thing for you to hurry back to finish. Have fun!"

Jesse's contract had been filed as her own. She hoped Mike wasn't in the office on Friday. She dialed his work number, but of course he wasn't in at—she glanced at her watch—5:00 A.M. on a Saturday. The beep sounded and she left the lawyer a message. "Hey, don't file that last artist agreement. We need to make some changes."

Then she called Mike's cell and left the same message. She had hoped he would answer, but maybe he slept more than she did.

She might be able to explain slipping away from Jesse without saying goodbye. It would be harder to explain stealing his first artist contract. Taylor watched as the road turned from city to desert as they headed through the outskirts of town toward the airport. She should turn around. Grab some coffee and donuts and pretend like she was just going for breakfast.

With your suitcase in tow? How would you explain that? You were afraid he'd try on your clothes? She stared at her reflection in the window. No, she'd already gone too far to go back. Even if she regretted the impulse to run. Now, later, and probably forever. The cab slowed next to the curb, and she gave the driver a twenty. Waving off her change, Taylor opened the taxi door and strode to the ticket counter, hoping for an easy transfer to an earlier flight.

Three hours later she was home in Boise. Taylor dropped her suitcase into her trunk, turned the car left instead of right toward home, and drove to Eagle, where her favorite hot springs spa was located. She knew the owner and hoped there was at least one room available. She wanted to hide. Hide and enjoy the services of Sally's best masseuse. She tossed her phone into the passenger seat. She'd turned off the cell as soon as she'd climbed on the plane. She couldn't talk to anyone until she got her head straight. She'd turn it back on Monday. If she decided to go in to work. The gallery was dark on Mondays, so technically she wouldn't be missed unless she didn't show on Tuesday.

But Brit would know. Taylor usually did payroll and the majority of paperwork on Mondays. So most of the time, Brit came in to help, or gossip. Mostly to gossip.

Taylor couldn't worry about that now. All she needed to do was get Jesse Sullivan out of her brain long enough to make some intelligent decisions. Decisions that weren't based on how amazing he'd made her feel last night, or how soft his caress had been. She'd had lovers in the past, she wasn't a saint. But she had never made love before. The experience with the other men had been sex. Fun, mind-blowing sex.

Last night with Jesse, she'd felt a connection. More than just their bodies joining.

Being with Jesse had overwhelmed her senses. She felt like their limbs had melted into each other, becoming one. She pulled her suitcase out of the trunk and stared at the cottage-style building situated close to the Boise River. Now she definitely knew that she needed some perspective. She was talking gibberish, like she was feeling a strong emotion. Like she was feeling love. For Jesse. She'd met the guy less than a month ago, so at the most, she was in lust. Not love. She decided her first stop would be the spinning room. She'd work this feeling out on a bike. And if that didn't work, she'd run.

She didn't want to think about what she'd have to do after running if Jesse Sullivan stayed in her head.

• • •

Two days later, Taylor snuck into the gallery, well rested with her head on straight. She felt ready to deal with all the bullcrap. As soon as Taylor walked in, Brit crossed the lobby to greet her. She took her arm and whispered, "Where have you been?" When Taylor hesitated, Brit took Taylor's purse and straightened Taylor's suit jacket. "Never mind. You can tell me later. You have a visitor in your office. I offered him coffee, but he declined."

Steeling herself, Taylor thought about the decision she'd made during her mud bath at the spa. No Jesse, no sex, nothing but business. She straightened her shoulders and opened the door to her office, her lie to Jesse already formulated in her mind. "Sorry about disappearing this weekend, I had gallery business."

"You disappointed me, Taylor. I thought maybe we'd catch a performance of the traveling ballet troupe in town." Mike sat in her chair, waving her into her own office. He held a hand over the phone's mouthpiece. "I'm on a call with some people who are very interested in investing in a gallery. One more substantial investment and I've solved your problem. You'll own your own business."

Not Jesse. Taylor set her planner on the desk and exhaled. She waved Mike out of her chair. "I won't be the owner. I'll just have more people telling me what I need to do."

He shook his head. "Everyone has a boss, Taylor." He focused on the call as he walked away, allowing her to slip into the chair he'd just vacated. He left the room, and Brit strolled in.

"So our new employee stood me up this weekend." Brit sat on the chair in front of Taylor's desk. She peeled a banana. "I hate to hit you with this first thing, but I thought you should know."

"Angie? She didn't show up for her shift? Did she at least call?" Taylor booted up her computer. She didn't need this, not today. Jesse would be sauntering in that door at any moment wanting to know why she had disappeared. Despite two days of contemplation at the spa, she hadn't come up with what she wanted to say. A good excuse for her behavior.

"She called, said she wasn't feeling well, and that she'd be in on Tuesday." Brit shook her head. "I hope she won't flake out—I kind of like having her around. It gives me more time to work on the upcoming exhibits without having to stay late every night."

Mike came back into the office and slid his phone into his pocket. "What's going on?"

Taylor clicked open her e-mail program and saw an e-mail from Jesse. She clicked the program shut. She'd deal with it once her office wasn't the gathering spot. "Nothing's going on, Mike. Angie just called in sick, that's all. People get sick."

Mike put his hand on the chair where Brit sat. "You know, there's no protection for employees under federal law until they've been on the payroll for a year. Maybe firing her now would make Jesse reconsider buying the gallery? They seem to be a pretty tight family."

Taylor's stomach soured at the thought. Just how low would she have to stoop to save the gallery? She shook her head. "We're not playing dirty. Just see if you can find investors. If we don't put together a package by the end of the week, I'll resign myself to the sale."

"But Taylor, I think there's an opportunity here." Mike stepped closer to the desk. "Your folks will come around. I know they really don't want to sell. You know your mom can be a bit of a wild card."

She looked at the glee in Mike's eyes. Had he always been this determined? Would he do anything, or hurt anyone to win? She leaned back in her chair. "Mike, just leave. I'm not playing your game."

Brit must have seen the pain in Taylor's eyes, because she stood and took Mike's arm. "Taylor needs some time alone." Mike didn't fight; he let Brit walk him to the door. When she returned to the office, she didn't come in, opting instead to lean against the doorframe.

"What?" Taylor pulled the pile of mail closer and started ripping open envelopes.

Brit didn't answer. Finally Taylor looked up at her friend and sighed.

"What have I started?" She set the torn envelope down on her desk.

This time, Brit answered her. "I don't know. Mike seems like he's more invested in saving the gallery than you are. I haven't seen him act like that since you dumped him freshman year."

Taylor cocked her head and stared at Brit. "I don't remember dating Mike."

Brit smiled sadly. "You thought you were just going to the game with a group of friends. However, Mike never got over it. When he got up the courage to ask you out again, you were already dating Ken."

"You can't be serious. That was years ago. There's no way Mike is interested in me. The business, yes. He's worked at the firm that handles the gallery and our family business since he left law school." Taylor thought about Mike's comment about the ballet. Sure, they'd gone places together, but she didn't consider that dating. The question was, did he? "I've never seen him that way. He's always just been Mike. A friend."

"History always comes back to bite us," Brit said. "Do you want some coffee? Some girl talk?"

"Coffee yes, talk no." Taylor glanced at her computer screen. She needed to find out what Jesse had written. Then she needed to talk to Angie and see if she was okay.

She waited for Brit to return with the cup and a filled carafe. "Close the door, please."

Brit started to say something, nodded instead, and clicked the door shut behind her.

Taylor stared at the door for a few seconds before returning to her laptop and opening Jesse's e-mail. She quickly read through the three lines. Short, to the point, and, surprisingly forgiving. *Sorry you couldn't stay. Hope everything is all right. Jesse.* It was like he'd read her fear the way he read the bulls he rode. Twisting left to keep her from bucking him off, he backed away. There was an implication—no, a promise—that he would call. When had she turned into a scared deer, needing to be herded toward the safety of the forest?

She sat at her desk for an hour, thinking about her next steps. She didn't want anyone leading her one way or the other. She could call her folks, but they were definitely in Camp Jesse. Mike, well, he wasn't the best person to bounce ideas off. And Brit, she was too close to the gallery to give her unbiased opinion. When had her life become all about the gallery? All about work?

A soft knock on the door broke Taylor out of her musing. Angie stood in the doorway, dressed in what must be a conservative outfit for her. She had on a bright purple suit. Under the suit, a creamy-white silk tank peeked out from behind a pile of gold jewelry. Even with Angie's caking layers of makeup, her skin looked pale and the woman seemed tired.

"Hey, come on in. Brit told me you were sick this weekend. Maybe you should have stayed home another day?" Taylor stood as Angie stomped in on platform leopard heels. Angie sunk into one of the chairs and leaned forward.

"I needed to come in. I can't just stay at home; I'll make myself crazy." Angie studied Taylor's face. "How was Wyoming?"

"Did you hear from Barb or Jesse?" Taylor waited for Angie's reaction.

Her eyebrows rose. "Both. Does that surprise you? We're kind of a close-knit bunch."

Taylor pulled out a bag of salt and vinegar chips she'd stashed in her desk drawer and tore it open. After pulling a handful out and setting them on a napkin, she offered the bag to Angie. When the woman grimaced and shook her head, Taylor frowned. "Seriously, maybe you *should* have stayed home another day. There's a flu bug going around."

Angie sighed and leaned back into the chair. "Give an old woman a break. I'm not stupid enough to come in if I were contagious or vomiting all over everything. I'm just dealing with some bad news. I'll be better tomorrow."

Taylor folded down the seal on the chip bag and put it away in the drawer. She wasn't fooling herself. The way she felt, the bag would be gone by closing. At least, if it was out of sight, she'd have to burn the few calories it took to drag it out of the drawer each time she got the craving. "I didn't say you were going to infect everyone."

"It was in your tone. Believe me, what I have isn't catching." Angie glanced around the office. "You don't believe in decorating much, do you?"

Taylor pressed her lips together and ate another chip before she answered. "I believe it's called minimalism."

"I think it's because you can't make up your mind. Have you ever claimed a spot as your own? This feels more like a man's office."

Taylor glanced around the office she'd inherited from her grandfather. Leather chairs, a large wooden desk, bookshelves filled with art books, and a worn, but usable, leather couch. "My grandfather must have decorated the room." She paused, seeing the furniture through new eyes. "I never even considered changing it."

"A woman steeped in tradition. No wonder Jesse's fallen for you. That boy always did want the Norman Rockwell kind of life."

"Jesse hasn't fallen for me," Taylor protested, but even as the words came out of her mouth, she knew they weren't true. It was too much. His love, his expectations. Even his trust in her, when all she was trying to do was keep him from buying the gallery.

"A mother knows." Angie tapped her blue-rimmed nails on the seat of the chair.

"Look, I'm not comfortable talking about my relationship, or my non-relationship, with your son. Did you want something?" Taylor opened the drawer and dumped out another handful of chips. *Stress-eat much?*

Angie seemed to squirm in her chair. "Actually, I need to tell you something. But you can't tell anyone. As my employer, I can hold you to that promise. No Barb. No Jesse. No one outside this office."

"I thought you were a close-knit bunch?" Taylor asked. She felt bad when her words reflected on Angie's face like the outline of a handprint after a hard slap. "Sorry, I'm being a bitch. Of course, you can tell me anything. And as long as it's not illegal, I promise, I won't tell anyone else."

Angie looked around the room again. "I would have liked your grandfather. I decorated my first house with the boys' dad a lot like this. Lots of wood and leather. Very masculine and country."

Taylor smiled as she followed Angie's gaze around the room. "He was an awesome man. Generous, giving, and he had the best laugh. I loved spending time here at the gallery with him when I was a little girl. He explained the pictures to me, then, after a while, he had me explain the pictures to him." Taylor laughed. "He was probably training me how to understand art, even as a child. Nevertheless, he said the gallery knew when someone loved it."

Angie nodded, the look in her eyes distant. "My grandfather worked on a farm in South Dakota. Dry farming. Praying for just the right amount of rain each year. Gone from sunup to sundown, only coming in to eat dinner at noon, then back out to the fields." Angie smiled at the memory. "He loved us grandkids. When we stayed with him in the summer, he would take my brother and me swimming on Saturdays down in the creek, where the water pooled under a big oak."

A small beep came through the laptop speakers announcing a new e-mail.

"Do you need to get that?" Angie sat forward in her chair. She looked like a rabbit poised to flee at any frightening movement.

"It can wait." Taylor threw away the oil spotted napkin and focused on Angie. "I know you didn't come in to tell me I needed to redecorate. What's going on?"

Angie studied her, and for a minute, Taylor thought she might just bolt. *Please, don't let this be about Jesse*, she prayed silently. She wasn't sure she could be strong enough to hold her feelings back right now. Mike had the financing in place, and she'd be at least a partial owner of Main Street Gallery in a few weeks. All she had to do was keep Jesse from finding out. She owed it to her grandfather to keep the gallery in the family. He'd always called it the family legacy. If her parents weren't going to honor the man, she would.

Taylor watched as Angie pulled a tissue out of her purse and dabbed at her eyes. The minutes stretched as the silence grew. Finally, Angie pulled her shoulders straight, sat up, and looked directly at Taylor.

When she spoke, the words stunned Taylor. "I have breast cancer."

Chapter 12

Angie sat in the leather chair not looking at Taylor. "You can't tell the boys. I'm fine. Just a few procedures, tests, then I'll be back to normal."

Taylor felt like she'd been punched in the gut. "Angie, it's not like you need a dental cleaning. Cancer is serious. Jesse needs to know—family can help."

"You don't understand. I wasn't there for them when they were growing up. Not when James broke his arm or when Jesse got measles. Why should I ask them to sit with me?" Angie twirled her hair in her fingers. "I hope I don't lose my hair. I've heard that some people don't."

"They make great wigs now." Taylor reached for something positive to say.

Angie smiled. "I've always wanted to be a redhead. Maybe I'll try it out for a while." She stared out the window for a long time. "I'll need a few weeks after my surgery, then chemo days off. Other than that, I can work around the appointments. Sometimes, I might have to switch up my hours. Can you work around that?"

"Of course we can. But do you think you want to work?" Taylor thought about the next few weeks. "We typically close for a couple weeks in July to reset for the year. We could move that up to match your surgery schedule. That way you won't miss too much time."

Angie smiled. "Whatever you want. I'll have a date soon. I'm serious about the boys. If we can keep this just between us, I'd appreciate it."

Taylor stood and walked around the desk, sitting in the chair next to Angie. "I'll respect your wishes, but just know, if you need anything, I'm here."

She patted Taylor's hand. "You're sweet, but I've always been independent. I got through most of my life alone; I can do this better by myself. I don't want to worry about how the boys are feeling, or what my new boss thinks about my hairstyle."

Taylor stayed in the chair for a while after Angie left. One more reason to call this thing with Jesse off. She'd never be able to keep a secret this big from someone she loved. Slept with, she amended. Not love; not yet.

Keep telling yourself that.

• • •

Jesse stood in his studio. He'd rented the place a year ago in order to keep his artwork a secret from his brother and Angie. Of course, James hardly ever came down to the Boise ranch, preferring to spend his time in Shawnee at the hot springs with Lizzie. Jesse could have set up a place in the barn, the loft, or even the back shed. Still he wanted a place to call his own.

Eventually, he had to buy a place. Just, not yet. With this deal on the art gallery almost complete, Jesse felt like he'd taken enough risk for now. Besides, the light came into his studio first thing in the morning. The suite was on one of the top floors of an old warehouse overlooking the Boise River. He had a small balcony where he could sit and watch people walk and bike down the greenbelt. He spent a lot of time sitting on the balcony when his head was too full to paint.

Like today.

All he could think of was the way Taylor had looked that night, staring into his eyes as they'd made love. Like she couldn't believe he was there. Hell, he couldn't believe they were together. When he'd woken up and rolled over, he'd found her side of the bed empty. Even now, he could feel the pain of that moment. Obviously, she'd wanted to walk on the wild side.

He'd known girls like her before. They'd step out of their real life of dating business moguls, lawyers, and doctors to try a rodeo rider, a bad boy. He'd been her mistake. And she'd run as fast and as far as she could once she'd woken.

He hadn't been able to reach her for days. Today, he'd called the gallery and talked to his mom. She'd mentioned Taylor was in the office with her attorney. She was probably trying to find some way to keep him from buying the place.

He finished his beer and went back inside, picking up a paintbrush. He didn't work on the portrait of Taylor. Instead, he focused on a landscape—a place that wasn't anywhere except inside his head. A place he dreamed of finding someday.

The house he painted had a window with light shining through the pane, welcoming family and strangers alike. He painted the imaginary home he'd always wanted, yet never had.

His phone buzzed. Clicking his Bluetooth, he answered, "Talk to me."

"Is that any way to answer your phone?" Angie chided. "Where are you?"

"Where am I supposed to be?" He set the paintbrush into a jar of paint thinner. He was done. He studied the house he'd been painting. Taylor would love living there. Too bad it was as imaginary as their relationship.

"I was hoping you were home. I need some company tonight. I thought we might try out that new barbeque place out in Meridian." Angie sounded disappointed. "After I couldn't get settled at my apartment, I drove up here to get you."

"I'm not there." He pulled off his painting tank top and put his T-shirt back on.

She sighed. "Still in Wyoming, huh? I thought you sounded closer when I talked to you this afternoon. Maybe later this week?"

Jesse chuckled. "I'm not in Wyoming, I'm just not out at the ranch. Come into town and meet me at the Alibi. I'll be the one sitting at the bar drinking beer until you get there."

"And I'll be the designated driver," Angie teased. "Of course, with you, I usually am."

"Not true." He glanced around the studio; the afternoon light slipped over the floor and made its way toward the sliding glass doors to dump into the river.

"Sometimes it's true." Jesse heard Angie start up her car. "I'll see you in fifteen."

"Twenty, more likely." Jesse grabbed his keys out of his jeans pocket. "Love you, Mom."

He heard her slight intake of breath before she responded. "Love you, too."

He jogged down the stairs to the parking lot and out to his truck. He was ten minutes away from Alibi. He needed to get there first and chug down most of a beer so Angie wouldn't question where he'd really been when she'd called.

It wasn't like she didn't know his secret. She'd picked him up at class before. But he didn't think she realized how much time he really committed to learning the craft. Buying the gallery wasn't a whim like James believed. He felt called to the art world as much as he felt called to bull riding. It just felt right.

• • •

"Ready for another?" Tina, the evening bartender, leaned over the counter. She gave him a good look at her cleavage and the leopard-print bra that held in her girls. He'd gone there before, trying to ease the loneliness he'd felt over the years. Now he knew it would just be a distraction. The only woman he wanted was Taylor. And she saw him as a play toy. Karma sure had a funny way of slapping you across the face.

"Might as well. Angie's on her way to get me, and you know how that goes. She might get distracted, and I'll be here all night waiting." Jesse turned on a 100-watt smile he didn't feel. He glanced around the nearly empty bar. "Slow night?"

Tina grabbed a bottle out of the cooler and flipped the top off, setting it in front of him with a clunk. "Tuesdays are dead lately. The computer plant up the street is talking about layoffs, so people are staying home. Of course, once they find out if they're on the chopping block, they'll be back in, either way. People don't like uncertainty."

"I understand. I'm kind of in a period of change, myself." Jesse twisted the bottle around, peeling off a corner of the label. "I can handle almost anything. But when I know something's happening, and I don't know what it is, it's maddening."

Tina frowned and scooted her stool over near him. "You got troubles, Jesse? You always seem so put together, so successful. Hell, you're the poster child for sanity in this place."

"Sad statement on your patrons." Angie stood in the doorway, bright sunshine filling the bar for a moment and framing her body.

Jesse smiled; his mother knew how to make an entrance. He knew she felt conflicted, claiming her status as mom of her boys after so many years away. Deep down, Angie was still a Las Vegas-style diva. But she definitely had a heart of gold. Cliché or not. "Hey, Mom. Want one before we go?"

Angie took a deep breath and considered the offer. He thought she took way too long.

"Something wrong?" He put his hand on her back and felt her shaking. "Angie? You're scaring me."

She dug in her purse. "I didn't think she would do this." She thrust an envelope onto the bar and looked up at Tina. "Get me a beer. I don't think I can get through this story without some help."

Tina hurried to pull out a bottle of Angie's favorite ale. She left the two alone and headed to the other side of the room to her only other customer. The jukebox in the corner started playing an old Patsy Cline song, popular with the older clientele.

He looked at the envelope. "This is from the law offices Taylor uses for the gallery. Don't tell me they've found out about your sordid past."

"Not funny. Besides, I could pass any background check anyone would run. My ex took care of those types of problems." She put her hand on his. "Read the letter, then I'll explain. It will give me time to calm down."

Jesse opened the envelope, pulled out the letter, and quickly scanned the contents. "Wait, they're firing you? And kicking you off their insurance? How is that even possible? I thought people had a right to some extension of coverage. Some snake name."

"COBRA coverage. Only if you've worked there for a year. I'm still in the probationary period, so I don't have rights." Angie took a swig from her beer. "I can't believe Taylor would do this to me."

"Taylor fired you? What did you do?" Jesse felt conflicted. Taylor wouldn't fire Angie without cause, would she? Was this a reaction to their weekend? He didn't like this one bit.

Angie stared at him, he could see the wheels turning in her head, and finally, she'd made a decision. "I got sick and told her about it."

"Why would she fire you because you didn't feel well? What, you were late for a shift? This doesn't make a bit of sense." Fire burned in Jesse's chest. This wasn't about Angie, it was about him. The girl wouldn't get away with this; she could ignore him, but she wasn't going to treat his mom with this lack of respect.

"Jesse, I don't want James to know. Hell, I didn't want you to know. I figured I could get this done on my own, but I need that insurance." Angie took a cigarette pack out of her purse and lit one. The last bastions of the smokers were small dive bars like Alibi.

Dread filled Jesse's mind as he watched her stall. "Mom, what's going on?"

She took a puff of the cigarette, stared at it, and then put it out. "Need to stop at least one bad habit." She tried to smile.

"Mom?"

Angie turned in her chair. "I have breast cancer. I told Taylor yesterday about my condition, and how I needed some time off for the surgery. And today, she dismisses me. I've never gotten a 'Dear Jane, you're fired' letter before. Hell, she had to have called her lawyer as soon as I walked out of her office yesterday."

Jesse's head spun. He didn't know what to react to first: his mom's medical condition or the fact that Taylor had sucker punched her so effectively. He'd thought he was falling in love with her. What an idiot. He should have known. The wealthy think they're different, and Taylor grew up a spoiled princess in the art world. To her, he had never been anything more than the novelty bull rider who liked to dabble in making pictures.

"I need your help." Angie had tears falling down her face. "I thought I could do this on my own, but without a job or insurance, I don't know what to do."

Jesse pulled his mother into his arms and let her sob. He'd never seen her this upset or out of control. His voice was tight and quiet when he finally responded. "You don't worry. I'll talk to Taylor tomorrow and get this all cleared up. I'm sure it's a misunderstanding."

Angie sniffed and leaned away. Her mascara ran down her cheeks, and even in the darkened bar, she looked like a raccoon. "You think she'll change her mind? Hire me back?"

Jesse brushed a tear off his mother's face. "I know she will. Now go into the bathroom and fix this ..." He waved his hand over his own face. "Then, when you get out, we'll go to that restaurant you've been wanting to try. A good meal will make you feel better."

She laughed. "I might as well eat now while I can. I've heard that once the treatments start I'll be too tired to eat."

"Then let's get you fattened up for the duration." He kissed her cheek. "Don't worry. We'll get you through this, no problem."

Angie smiled as she slipped off her bar stool, and clicked toward the bathroom. "You still can't tell your brother."

He waited for her to close the door before he took out his phone. He speed-dialed his brother's number, and when the call was answered, he got right to the point. "I need you down here for a family meeting. Bring Lizzie, we might need her. I'll call Barb and Hunter when I get home tonight."

"What's going on?" James's voice mirrored his own, hard and tight.

Jesse watched the bathroom door, hoping to get off the phone before Angie returned. "Tomorrow. About ten?"

"We'll be there. Lizzie will call Barb." James paused and Jesse could hear his brother's unspoken question: *What have you gotten yourself into now, little brother?*

He almost wanted to laugh. "See you then."

Jesse slipped his phone into his jeans pocket and waved Tina over. "What's our tab? Time for some dinner."

Tina didn't even look at the page where she'd written down the beer orders since Jesse walked in. It wasn't like she'd been swamped with customers for the last thirty minutes. "Twelve dollars."

He handed her a twenty, and when she walked back with his change, he waved her off. "Yours."

She smiled and tucked it into the tip jar. "I can always count on you, Mr. Sullivan. Too bad most of the men who come in don't have your tipping expertise."

"I just know how it is to sing for your supper, so to speak." He frowned at the bathroom. Angie was taking too long just to fix her mascara. But then again, she did love her makeup. He smiled at Tina. "How're classes going? You about done with your degree?"

"One more year, then I'm kissing this place goodbye. My professor says she thinks I can get an internship at one of the accounting firms downtown." She glanced down at her silver sparkling tank and too-tight jeans. "I'm going to have to upgrade my work wardrobe just a tad."

"I don't know about that, dear. You should see the clothes the girls are wearing in the corporate world." Angie hitched her purse up on her shoulder. "You ready to go, cowboy?"

Jesse tipped the brim of his ball cap to Tina. "See you next time."

As they walked out into the bright sunshine, he could have sworn he heard a sigh come from the tough-as-nails bartender. He was really going to have to tread carefully here. He didn't want to lose his favorite watering hole over girl trouble.

Angie clicked open the doors on her car. "You want to ride with me, or follow?"

He was already opening the door to his truck. "I've got an early appointment tomorrow. I'll follow."

"Stubborn as the day is long."

He rolled down his window and leaned out, his arm resting on the doorframe. "Runs in the family." He motioned to her car. "Go on, I'll follow you."

He watched her pull out onto the street that would lead them to the freeway, and eventually, out to Meridian. He clicked on his phone and gave it a verbal command. "Call George."

George Baxter was part lawyer, part family friend, and a good old boy. Jesse had programmed George's number into the contact list just in case he ever needed him. He thought about how the day was progressing, and today seemed like that kind of day.

As soon as the line was connected, Jesse said, "There's a family meeting out at the ranch tomorrow at 10:00 a.m. When can you get there?"

George paused and Jesse could hear paper being flipped. "Nine-thirty?"

"Good enough."

The man on the other end asked, "Can you give me a hint about the problem? An indiscretion? Drunk and disorderly? Hiring a hit man?"

"Employment law and medical disabilities," Jesse growled.

A pause hung on the other end of the line. "That's not what I expected."

"Glad I can keep you guessing." Jesse turned the truck onto the freeway, stepping on the gas to keep up with his lead-footed mother. "See you tomorrow."

Chapter 13

"Definitely not our normal dining establishment." Mike glared at the waitress dressed in Daisy Dukes and a tied-up flannel shirt, showing both her midriff and cleavage.

Taylor smiled at the reaction and giggled. "I thought all men liked places like this." The new barbeque restaurant had opened with a flair last month. Taylor had heard the food was amazing, even if the waitstaff needed more fabric to their uniforms. When Mike had called an emergency dinner meeting, she'd suggested the place closest to her new gym.

Mike huffed. "Not me. I'd rather see women dressed to leave something to the imagination. When it's all out on display there's no mystery."

"Well, you're the one who just had to meet me for dinner tonight. My Pilates class starts at eight, so I had to be somewhere nearby if we were going to make this happen." Taylor glanced at the beer menu, then pushed it away. No need going to exercise tipsy. After the waitress had taken their order and brought her a large water and a cup of herbal tea, Taylor leaned back and looked at her companion. He was staring straight at her, clearly trying not to let his eyes be tempted by the young, buxom women floating around their table.

He took a sip of his whisky. "There really has to be somewhere else we can eat."

Taylor sighed. "What do you want, Mike? I think we both know that our relationship is purely business casual. There was never any heat between the two of us."

"That's not true. Remember that kiss last New Year's Eve?" He looked like a puppy that just had his favorite chew toy taken away forever.

"Heat of the moment, not real heat." Taylor sighed. "Look, I don't want to hurt you, but I'm not interested in anything but a friendship. And if you're seeing us being more than that, we need to stop being friends."

"I don't agree." He held up his hand to stop Taylor's next words. "But if that's how you're feeling, I won't push. We'll just be friends."

Taylor reached over and patted the top of his hand. "Thank you."

"Well, isn't this cozy?" Jesse stood in front of her, staring at her hand on Mike's. She resisted the urge to jerk it back. Instead, she removed her hand slowly and put it under the table.

"Hi, Jesse. I didn't expect to see you tonight." Taylor glanced around the room looking for his date. Finally, her eyes landed on Angie, who quickly turned her head. Had she been crying? What was going on?

"Mom asked me not to make a scene, and I won't, for her sake." Jesse leaned closer to her, whispering his next words into her ear. "But you and your lawyer buddy aren't getting away with this. As soon as the ink's dry on the contract to buy the gallery, you're out on your pretty little butt."

Taylor jerked away. "Get away with what? What are you talking about?"

Jesse hadn't stayed for a response. He was already heading to Angie's table, his back to Taylor and Mike.

"What was that all about?" Mike asked.

Taylor shook her head, damning the tears filling up behind her eyes. She wouldn't cry—not here, not in public, and certainly not over Jesse Sullivan. "Nothing."

"Sounds like the bull rider is high on something. Probably steroids. I hear they're pretty rampant throughout the circuit."

She shook her head. "Stop. This isn't Jesse's fault." *It's mine.* But she couldn't tell Mike, a man who was most certainly in love with her, that she'd snuck out of Jesse's bed this weekend like a prostitute already paid for the deed. "Let's just eat."

When she finished her dinner, Jesse and Angie were gone from the dining room. Maybe Angie had changed her mind and told her youngest son about the cancer. Jesse would be a rock for her. She just hoped Angie's way would be lit brightly, and she'd come through the other side healthy and cured.

She picked up her purse and threw a couple twenties down for the waitress.

Mike picked the money up and pushed it back into her hand. "I'll bill the office. I was going to talk business tonight, but I think it should wait until tomorrow. I'll stop by the gallery late morning."

Taylor nodded. "I'll be there." She excused herself and turned toward the restroom.

When she returned to the dining room, Mike was gone and the table had already been cleared. She checked her watch and pulled her tote closer. She had five minutes to walk to class and get changed. The way her stomach was rolling, she probably should just skip tonight.

She was still arguing with herself when she saw Jesse leaning against his truck, watching her. Determined, she squared her shoulders, unwilling to go on the defensive. If he wanted to fight, they'd do it on her terms. She pointed a finger at him. "What did you think you were doing in there? Mike is my lawyer, nothing more. And your fight is with me, not him."

"I beg to differ. His name is on the letter." Jesse tipped his hat further back on his head. "He's just as much to blame as you are. Although, I think you're cold-hearted, from what Angie told me."

"I am not cold-hearted," she said, angrily, before his words sunk in. "Wait, what are you talking about? What's Angie got to do with this?"

He stood up straight, fury burning his cheeks a flame red. And heaven help her, she wanted him. Hot and angry, the boy was as sexy as he had been when he'd looked at her with lust. Or love. Her brain changed the descriptor without her permission. She took a step forward, but caught herself before she'd gone running into his arms.

He reached into the cab of the truck and grabbed a piece of paper. "Don't play dumb-blond with me." Jesse crumbled the page in his hand. "Are you really that heartless?"

"What's that?" Taylor tried to see what was written on the page, but Jesse wouldn't hold still.

"It's the letter you had your henchman send to my mom. What did that cost you? Dinner and some extracurricular activities later tonight?" His gaze flowed up and down her body. "I guess you're good enough to sell it."

Any touch of positive emotion she'd felt at seeing Jesse escaped her as his words hit her like a sucker punch. "You are nuts. I don't know what you're talking about, but I don't care."

"Of course not. You're punishing Mom for what went on this weekend. Hell, I would have sworn you were having fun, too." Jesse didn't meet her eyes. "At least, until I woke up alone in that hotel room with no note, no goodbye. You could have left some money on the table, and at least I would have understood. Or was this all payback from Ontario?"

"I …" Taylor paused. What could she say? *I did enjoy myself? I fell in love, so I ran? You're too good for me?* No, there wasn't anything she could say to redeem her actions that night. She had decided their fate the minute she'd run. "I really don't know why you're so upset about this. I had to catch an early flight back. Gallery business."

This time, Jesse looked at her. She felt his eyes burning into her soul, and she almost cringed as she realized he knew the lie. "I called Brit on Sunday. She didn't know where you were. Unless your gallery business involved spending some one-on-one time with Mikey."

"It's not any of your business who I spend time with." She regretted the words as soon as she said them. Jesse nodded, knowingly. Why wasn't she just telling him she was confused, that she hid from everyone at the spa? Then the reason hit her: she didn't want to appear weak. She didn't want him to know that she needed him. She'd been strong and independent her entire life. Like Angie. Leaning on a man, especially one like Jesse, just wasn't in the cards for her. She didn't want to give in to anyone.

"Bingo." Jesse crumpled the paper in his hand tighter. "I should have seen that coming. Girls like you don't fall for bull riders. They like their men more metrosexual. They like doctors and … lawyers." The word spit out of him like a cuss word.

Taylor bit her lip. "Look, we had fun. Can't we leave it at that?"

For a minute, she thought he was going to try to convince her it wasn't just fun. He took a half step forward, then sighed and climbed into his truck. "Fair warning, I'm going to destroy you. After we sign the contract for the gallery, you're out of a job. I'm going to tell every gallery owner in the area how you treat employees. They may hire you, or not. Of course, you always have Mike to take you in."

"Go to hell, Jesse Sullivan."

He started the truck and tipped his hat. "Not a problem."

She stared after him as he gunned the truck and sped down the street. She yelled after him. "I hope you get a ticket."

A man walking by on the sidewalk chuckled.

Taylor turned and stared, hoping to make him at least turn his head away from her.

"Lovers' quarrels are the best. Makes making up all the sweeter." He squeezed the hand of a lady walking next to him. "Isn't that right, dear?"

She didn't wait for the woman's answer; instead, she turned away from the direction of the gym where she had class. She didn't want to go home and run into her parents. She didn't want to just drive. She wanted a drink.

Taylor took her cell out of her purse and punched Brit's number. When the call was answered, she didn't wait for a greeting. "You still got a bottle of tequila at your place?"

• • •

Jesse drove on autopilot up to the ranch above Boise. He wanted to hit something. He wanted to kill someone. He wanted to turn the world back three years, to before Angie had come into their lives. Knowing you might have a mom somewhere out there who didn't give a crap was much better than knowing she might be dying of cancer. And now, he'd broken up with Taylor too.

Man, how could he have read her so wrong? Usually, he had a knack for picking out the mean girls. The ones who liked the game more than being in love. He'd played with a few before, but he'd never given away his heart to that type. Until now.

Angie's leaving when he and James were kids had taught him one thing. Girls never stay. He'd fooled himself into thinking that Taylor was different. She'd had a normal childhood, a cool mom, but deep down, women were all the same. They were always looking for the best option for their future husband. Hell, she probably had used sex just to get close to him and keep track of information on the gallery sale. If she thought she'd keep her job now, she was a bigger fool than he'd ever been.

He sped the truck a little too fast on the winding road up the mountain, fishtailing on a corner. Thank God, no vehicle was coming down the road around that corner. He took a breath and slowed the truck. No use driving into the river running next to the road just because of a girl. He'd get over this one.

Idiot. He should have seen this coming. He thought of the portrait of her in his studio downtown. The soft curves of her body and the sparkle in her eyes, as if she had a secret. A freaking Mona Lisa smile.

He parked the truck in front of the ranch house next to Angie's BMW. He should have known she'd head up here once he sent her home from the restaurant. He slammed the truck door and stomped into the house. "What are you doing here?"

"Sit down and have a drink." Angie sat in the living room in front of the lit fireplace. Even though it was still warm outside, the cabin felt welcoming, not stifling.

"I don't want to talk," Jesse said as he grabbed a beer out of the silver bucket filled with ice and longnecks.

Angie stared into the fire. "Me neither."

He slipped into the leather recliner next to the sofa. After a few minutes, he said, "You're going to be fine. And you're going back to work as soon as the gallery deal is done. In the meantime, we'll figure something out."

Angie nodded distractedly. "You know, I did love your father. I wish I'd been smarter back then. I had everything I ever needed in that little cabin."

"Can't change the past," Jesse said, even though, on the drive here, that had been exactly what was on his mind. Changing his past, so this present would have never happened.

"Your father used to set a fire once a week just so we could sit together and talk." Angie smiled. "When you boys got old enough, we'd make hot dogs for dinner those nights, and roast marshmallows later."

"I remember. James always said I was going to burn my marshmallow holding it too close to the flame." Jesse smiled at the memory.

"And he was right, you always did. Then James would give you his when you cried. That boy was Mr. Responsibility from day one."

"He took care of me for years. Years longer than I should have let him." Jesse took a swig of his beer. "I almost messed up him and Lizzie."

"True love always wins, no matter what the obstacles." Angie sat her drink down and stared at him. "Speaking of, you're in love with that girl."

Jesse shook his head. "Doesn't matter. She's not in love with me."

"Are you sure about that?" Angie's voice was soft.

Jesse thought about the fight less than an hour ago. "When she told me to go to hell, I think she was pretty sure about her feelings."

A soft laugh came from his mother. "Oh, honey, that just tells you how deep her emotions run. I'd be more worried if she'd just said goodbye without any heat. Anger requires deep passion."

Jesse sipped his beer, thinking about his mother's words. "Then the girl must be head over heels for me, because I've never seen her that mad." His lips curve into a small smile. "But it doesn't matter. She burned you. That's reason enough to end the relationship, for me."

"Don't use me as an excuse, Jesse Sullivan. You've been running from love your entire life. I'm not a fool. I know why." Angie sighed. "It was me. Maybe that's why I'm sick: paying for my past transgressions. You think that's what causes cancers? Little bits of life where you make the wrong decision, and the regrets fester into cancer years later?"

Jesse stood from his chair and went to sit by Angie. He put his arm around her and she laid her head on his shoulder. "No, nothing you did caused this." He paused. "Except, maybe, the booze and cigarettes. You giving up smoking?"

He felt her sigh. "I've got the patch on now. I started a week ago, right after I saw the doctor."

"Good girl."

Angie sat up and took a sip of her drink. "The doctor said to stop drinking too, but one fight at a time, right?"

He smiled. "You can do anything."

"It's not fair that the one time I really need a cigarette, I can't have one." Angie stared into the fire. "Life sure throws you some curveballs at times."

That it does. He wondered how pissed she was going to be when the family posse showed up tomorrow. Of course, she'd get over it. Eventually. For once in their lives, they were going to stand together in the bad times. No more lying or running away. *Watch out, cancer,* he thought as he watched his mother in the firelight. *We're coming after you, and Sullivans always win.*

Chapter 14

Lizzie and Barb had started cooking a late breakfast when Angie walked through the door wrapped in a pink fluffy robe and feather slippers. At first, her face lit up and she glanced around the room. "What's going on? Did you bring the kids with you?"

When everyone looked at Jesse, realization hit Angie, and her lips tightened.

"Angie, it's time to talk." Jesse stood up and kissed her on one cheek, handing her a cup of coffee.

She turned on him, her eyes wide with anger. In a low voice she said, "I told you not to mention this."

He led her to the table and pulled out a chair. "Sit down. We have some things to discuss."

She sat and glanced around the room. She smoothed hair with her hands when she saw George Baxter, the family lawyer, sitting next to James. "You might have warned me to dress up before meeting you all like this."

James laughed. "You look fine." He reached over and covered her hand with his own. "I'm sorry about this."

Jesse could see the tears fill Angie's eyes as she nodded. Damn, she was trying to be cool, but he knew their concern touched her. "First things, first. We need to make a schedule." He tapped a notebook and a calendar. When's your next doctor appointment?"

"Wednesday, with the surgeon, but ..." Angie was cut off by Barb.

"I'll take that appointment and talk to that doctor to get an idea of what's coming next." Barb tapped the appointment into her phone. "What time should I pick you up?"

"I really don't need help." Angie shook her head and scowled at Jesse. "This is why I didn't want you to know. I don't want to be a bother."

The gathering around the table glanced at James. "Mom, you're not a bother. We're family and we're going to fight this together. Don't start pointing your finger at me. I'm not calling you Angie anymore. You're my mother. Get used to it."

Angie wiped the tears from her eyes. "Okay, then. I never could talk you boys out of something once you got your minds made up."

"So what time do I pick you up?" Barb asked.

They discussed what the doctors had already told Angie, and filled their calendars with appointments and meetings. Lizzie and James decided to move down from the mountain back into the ranch house.

"I'm not sure you'll be getting much rest once the twins and JR arrive. Those boys love their grandma." Lizzie smiled as she put a basket of cinnamon rolls on the table.

"I think they'll be exactly what I need during my bad days." Angie took a roll and broke it apart. "So are we done beating this thing to death?"

"One more problem: your health insurance from the gallery." George looked grim. "I'm not sure what I can do now, but as soon as Jesse signs the purchase contract we'll get you back on the policy. Good news is that the insurance company cannot reject you on a pre-existing clause anymore. Can you delay the surgery until the sale is finalized?"

"No." James's answer came first. "We'll hire her on at the agency and get her coverage today." He glanced at Barb. "We can do that, right?"

She shook her head. "Even if we hire her, there's a ninety day waiting period on our policy. That's why I keep the riders on the insurance year-round instead of just during the rodeo season. It costs us more, but the guys are protected."

George looked at Jesse. "I'll go talk to this Taylor girl and see if we can get her to change her mind. The sale will be finalized in the next thirty days or so. Typically, management doesn't make big changes while things like this are pending. I don't know what she was thinking."

Everyone's gaze fell on Jesse. The room went silent as he struggled with the decision. Finally, he put Angie's needs in front of his own anger. What harm could it do to see Taylor again? "I'll go with you."

• • •

Taylor's head pounded. She couldn't believe she was even walking, considering the number of shots she'd pounded back last night. Salt, tequila, lemon, shudder. Rinse and repeat. At least she'd stopped crying about the fight with Jesse. Until she was truly good and drunk—then the blues hit harder than she'd ever felt them before. She needed to change her coping mechanisms, or she'd find herself in an intervention meeting faster than her folks could say, "move out of our house."

She pulled out the file with the condo information. She'd planned on buying the place next year by using her savings and income from the gallery. With the gallery being sold, and her job no longer secure, she wondered if she should shelve the idea in case the next step in her career wasn't here in Boise. All because she'd clung to some desperate idea that she had to uphold the family name. She touched the pictures of the model kitchen. Granite counter tops, walnut cupboards, and, more important, a gas stove. She could see herself living there, making pastas and pastries. Making breakfast when Jesse stayed over, his arms surrounding her, kissing her neck as she took the omelet makings out of the stainless steel refrigerator. She shook away the fantasy. She'd shut that door when she'd left Wyoming, doing her cross-state walk of shame.

Frowning, she replayed the argument back in her mind. Jesse had been mad about her being out with Mike. As if there was something going on there—ha. But he'd said something else, too. He'd said that she'd hurt Angie. Maybe Jesse had found out about Angie's health condition and blamed Taylor for not telling him first.

That didn't sound right. Jesse was mad about a letter. She could see the crumpled paper in his hand as he railed last night.

Taylor buzzed Brit, who was watching the front desk.

"Hey, you feeling better? Want some more coffee?" Brit sounded fine. Like she hadn't matched Taylor shot-for-shot last night. Taylor hated her for it, but only just a bit.

"Coffee would be good," she said. "Hey, is Angie in yet?"

There was a pause. "I'll bring a cup in. And no, she hasn't shown. Do you want me to call her?"

"No." Taylor opened her computer, looking for Angie's cell number. She dialed the number and got her voicemail. When Angie's prerecorded message ended, she left a brief message. "Call me. It's Taylor."

As Brit came into the room, she nodded to the phone. "Didn't reach her?"

"She said something yesterday about needing some time off. Maybe I didn't write down the dates right." Taylor sipped the black liquid like it was a healing potion.

Brit slipped into one of the guest chairs. "I was going to ask you what you guys were talking about. You were in here a long time. Mike stopped by and waited for a while, but then he took out of here like a shot."

"Wait. Mike was here when I was talking to Angie?" Taylor frowned; he hadn't mentioned that last night. The guy was beginning to feel like a creepy stalker instead of a concerned lawyer. Maybe it was better that the gallery was being sold. This way, she could cut her ties with Mike without hurting his feelings any more than she had last night.

Brit didn't seem concerned, though. "He watched the front for me while I took a bathroom break, but he took off when I came back. Said he'd talk to you later."

"Weird." Taylor glanced around the office. "Well, I guess in a few weeks this will be Jesse's office. Has he said anything about keeping you on? You know, you don't have to leave just because I'm persona non gratis around here."

Brit shrugged. "Doesn't matter one way or the other. But no, he hasn't talked to me. I'm surprised he kicked you to the curb. You want to tell me what really happened in Wyoming?"

Taylor leaned back, tapping a pen on her grandfather's desk. "I screwed it up. Have I always been a runner?"

Her friend laughed. "You've never let anyone get this close before, so it's hard to say. I can count on one hand the number of guys you've dated seriously, and that includes Jesse. Me, on the other hand, I'm a free spirit."

"Is that what they call it?" Taylor felt her lips curl. Talking to Brit always made her feel better.

"Depends on who 'they' are." Brit made air quotes with her fingertips. "My last boyfriend called me a slut when we broke up."

"He was a jerk."

The front doorbell rang and Brit stood, a wicked smile on her face. "Doesn't mean I wasn't a slut."

"Silly," Taylor called after her friend as she left. Relationships were too hard. Art was easy. You found something you loved and bought it. You found things other people might love, and bought them. If they didn't sell, then you were wrong. Love should be that easy.

A knock on the door brought her out of her musing. She looked up, half expecting Angie to be standing there in one of her wild outfits. Instead, Brit stood in the doorway, her face lined with worry. "What's up?" Taylor asked.

"Jesse and his lawyer are here. Do you feel up to talking to them?" Brit lowered her voice. "Should I call Mike and have him come over before you meet with them?"

"No. I mean, don't call Mike. I'm sure this is just something about the sale and my imminent departure. Send them in." Taylor glanced at her reflection in the monitor, hoping she didn't look as bad as she felt. "Stupid," she said to herself. What did she care how she looked? Jesse had broken up with her last night. No need to pretend she hadn't been upset. She took a deep breath and stood as the two men walked into the office.

"Thank you for seeing us," the older man said. "I don't think we've met before. George Baxter. I'm the Sullivan family lawyer."

Taylor shook his hand and motioned to the two guest chairs in front of her desk. "Family lawyer? I assumed you were here about the gallery sale contract."

A look passed between Jesse and George. "I handle their business issues, as well. Although this isn't about the sale; we've come to ask for a favor."

"I don't understand." Taylor ignored the lawyer and focused on Jesse. "After your tirade last night, you want a favor from me?"

Jesse wouldn't meet her gaze.

George spoke again. "Miss DeMarco, we are here on behalf of Angie."

Fear shot through her. "Oh my God, is she all right? I tried to call her just now. Is that why she didn't come in to work?"

This time Jesse didn't hold back. "Like you care? Like you were expecting her?"

Taylor's hands shot up in frustration. "Seriously, Jesse, get over yourself. Just because I didn't stay and cuddle after we made love the other night, doesn't mean I don't care about Angie. Why isn't she here?"

George put a hand on Jesse's arm, a gesture encouraging him to be silent. Now she was really worried. But she'd promised Angie she wouldn't be the one who told Jesse. Maybe they didn't know about her condition. If she was in the hospital, Taylor needed to say something. Her mind whirled as the two men sat quietly in front of her. Finally, Jesse nodded and the lawyer turned toward her.

"With the gallery sale in the final stages, we had hoped you wouldn't make any staffing changes." The man opened a briefcase and pulled out a pile of papers. "We're willing to make some concessions in exchange for this request."

Taylor glanced down at the page on top of the pile he had set in front of her. "I'm confused. What are we talking about? Where's Angie?"

George took a crumbled sheet of paper from his suit pocket. "Angie received this yesterday by courier. You didn't know?"

Taylor breathed a sigh of relief. This wasn't about the cancer. There was something else going on. Probably some issue from Angie's wild past coming back to haunt her. Taylor bit back a smile, wondering what trouble the woman had gotten herself into now. She was beginning to really enjoy working with the unpredictable Sullivan clan. Unfortunately, that was almost over due to her inability to keep her relationship with the new owner professional. The desire to smile left her, and she took the page from George.

Mike's law firm's letterhead struck her first. *Oh, man, this can't be good.* She skimmed the letter releasing Angie from employment with the gallery and wishing her safe travels. She pushed the letter back to the lawyer. No wonder Jesse was hot. Mike must have overheard her and Angie's conversation and taken it upon himself to solve the problem.

She thought about his call yesterday for dinner. He had to talk to her. Of course, once she'd misinterpreted the meeting and told him she just wasn't into him, this subject hadn't come up. It wasn't the first time Mike had acted on his own rather than at her direction. Unless he'd called Dad and got his permission. She had calls to make.

"I didn't authorize this termination. As long as I'm gallery director, Angie has a job here." She glared at Jesse whose eyes widened. "Of course, your client has made it very clear I'm not being asked to stay on during the transition, so I can't make any promises for after the contract is settled."

George shot a glance at Jesse, who, to Taylor's amusement, had the grace to look sheepish. "So she will continue on your insurance during the transition?"

Taylor stared at the two, wondering what they knew. Obviously, Angie had told them enough that they were fighting for her job and health insurance. Still, no one had said the word cancer, and it wasn't going to come out of her mouth before she knew exactly what Angie had said.

Taylor tapped her finger on the desk. "This letter was a mistake. I didn't authorize it. And if my father did, he will reverse the decision as soon as I talk to him." She stared at Jesse, but her words were aimed at the lawyer. "Please tell Angie to return to her normal schedule and that everything we discussed yesterday is still in place."

George nodded toward the stack of papers he'd set on the desk. "You don't want to read our offer?"

Taylor shook her head. "There's no need. This was a big misunderstanding on the gallery's part. Angie is a vital and important member of our staff, and we need her here. She can take the day off, but the two of us will talk in the morning when she comes in for her shift." She pushed the stack of papers back to George. "This is between Angie and me. There's no need for lawyers."

"You started it," Jesse said.

Taylor saw George squeeze his client's shoulder while he responded. "Now, Jesse, Ms. DeMarco has just explained this was a terrible misunderstanding." He stood, pulling Jesse up out of his chair as well. "Thank you for seeing us. I'm sure Angie will be overjoyed at the news."

Taylor felt tears fill in her eyes, but swallowed hard when she saw Jesse frown in confusion. Overjoyed wasn't a feeling she believed Angie would be having for a long time. At least, not until the doctor pronounced her cured, which could be many years from now.

She was going to kill Mike. If he'd gone behind her back to her dad …? Fury consumed her, but she had to keep it together for a few more minutes. She had to wait until Jesse and his hired gun were out of the room. She'd thought the fight last night was about their relationship. But no, he was sticking up for his mother.

The tears threatened again, but she pushed them away and stood, watching George stuff the paperwork back into his briefcase. Jesse might think she was a dragon lady, but she didn't have to act like it.

She held her hand out to George to conclude their discussion. "Thank you for clarifying this mess. It's nice to have a rational conversation with someone."

• • •

Jesse sat quietly while George pulled the car away from the curb. He saw the look his friend gave him, but turned away to stare out the window.

"You can't blame her, Jesse." George maneuvered the car out of downtown's main streets. They got on the highway heading toward the ranch to deliver the good news to the crew. "Sounds like her lawyer went rogue on her. I'd hate to be in his shoes when she calls him."

Jesse thought about what he'd seen last night at the restaurant. Taylor had looked focused, tapping the table, relaying something serious to Mike, who looked like a wounded bunny. Until Jesse went over and made a scene. The bastard had looked happy then. *No*, Jesse corrected himself, *hopeful*. Jesse's outburst had made the guy look hopeful. Had Taylor been telling the jerk she wasn't interested? And Jesse had misinterpreted the conversation?

"I wish she'd at least looked at the papers you drew up." Jesse sighed. "I'm going to have to fix my mistakes all on my own, huh?"

George chuckled. "Typically, that's how life works. You make the mess, you clean it up. But it was a good strategy. I'm sure she'll work with you on this. The girl seems to have a good head on her shoulders for business."

Jesse glanced at his watch. "I'm flying out again tomorrow to meet with sponsors. Can you work on fast-tracking this sale? I'd like to get the contracts signed next week when I get back."

"Getting antsy to take on a new enterprise?" George turned the vehicle onto the road that would take them to the ranch. "When are you announcing your retirement?"

Jesse sighed. "Barb wants me to wait until December, after the Vegas finals. I'd rather walk away today."

"Barb knows what she's doing. Besides, if you win, you might be able to keep some of those merchandising contracts for a few years."

Jesse stared out the window, not seeing the pine trees and forestland surrounding the road. "That's what she tells me. George, you ever just get tired?"

"Every night, but I don't think that's what you're talking about. This thing with Angie got you spooked? People live through cancer all the time. And if her doctors caught it early …"

Jesse held his hand up. "Can't talk about Angie right now. Just can't. But what I was thinking about was always being 'on.' I'm

The Bull Rider's Keeper

not a real person; I'm the bull rider. Sometimes that gets into your head, you know?"

George parked in front of the cabin behind the rows of cars that had arrived for the emergency family meeting. He turned off the engine and looked at Jesse. "You've never just been the bull rider to the people who really matter. You've been Jesse. And those are the people you have to hold close while you're transitioning. I won't blow smoke at you—you're going to have a tough time letting go of the limelight. But you can do it."

"Thanks." Jesse paused for a second, his hand on the door handle and his gaze on the cabin.

"I'm one of those people in your corner. So any time you need to talk, call me. I won't even charge you the standard billable hour rate for the call."

Jesse chuckled. "Glad to know."

The men walked up to the ranch house to give everyone the good news. Angie's job and insurance status were intact. That should have made Jesse feel better, but a black cloud still weighed heavily on his heart. He needed to correct his mistake before he lost the chance forever.

Chapter 15

A red-faced Mike sat in the leather chair in front of Taylor's desk. Her father sat in the chair across from Mike. The lawyer pounded the desk. "You aren't thinking this through. Her condition could raise your premiums. Do you want to lose your policy completely?"

"What I want is a lawyer who advises me, not runs to my father to go over my head every time he overhears a conversation." Taylor had already talked to her dad. Mike had made it seem like Taylor was on board with the firing of Angie. When they'd met, Taylor had told her father the entire truth. That way Mike couldn't throw her under the bus. Like he was doing.

Mike changed his tactic, turning to Rich DeMarco. "Sir, you have to realize what I did was for the good of the gallery. If Taylor expects to get the backing in place to force a sale to her, rather than this cowboy, she needs a strong package. And having the cowboy's mother there wasn't helping her proposal."

Taylor bristled, but saw her father's hand motioning her to calm down. Before the meeting, Taylor and her dad had agreed on a plan. Now Taylor just had to keep her cool while Rich worked it out.

"We appreciate your valuable advice over the years, but I agree with Taylor, you stepped over the line with this action. I'm afraid we won't need your services any longer." He pushed a business card toward Mike. "Please transfer our company and personal files over to Samantha Jones at this address. She's now our attorney."

Mike's eyes widened. "You're firing me? Over this?"

"According to our new attorney, you're lucky we aren't filing charges against you with the law board. But I convinced her that you were a longtime family friend and, as such, probably had our best interest at heart." Taylor leaned back in her chair, waiting for the reaction.

She didn't have to wait long.

"This is because you're sleeping with him. Taylor, he's a player. You don't know how many women he's had in his bed." Mike turned his attention on her. "You're just the flavor of the month."

That stung for a few seconds, but she knew Mike was hurt and lashing out. Hadn't she thought the same thing about Jesse? Now Mike had to go explain to the partners at his firm why he'd lost the DeMarco family and the gallery's business. That conversation wouldn't be pleasant; not at all.

"My personal relationships have nothing to do with this decision. I'm sorry, but your services are no longer needed." She stared at him, waiting for him to leave.

"You are cold-hearted. All I ever wanted was to help you, even when you came up with this crazy scheme." Mike stood. "I'll send over my final bill this afternoon."

He walked toward the door and her father called after him. "If you're smart, you won't be charging us for that problem yesterday."

Mike didn't answer, slamming the door as his farewell message. Taylor sighed and looked at her father. "Thanks for being here, Dad. I can't believe he even pulled something like this. I was mortified when Jesse and the lawyer showed up yesterday."

Her dad stood and held his arm out. "I think you need a hug." She fell into his arms and held back her tears. She wasn't sure why she felt like crying. *Pick a topic*, she thought. Jesse, Angie, Mike's betrayal, losing her job at the gallery ... it could be any or all of the above.

He sat her down in one of the chairs. "We do have to clear something up, though. If you want to buy the gallery, we won't sell to him. Your mom and I thought you'd be pleased with having the freedom to travel and explore the world. We didn't want you to feel stuck here in Boise, running a small gallery."

Here was her chance. She could stop this entire problem with one word. Well, three. *Don't sell to Jesse.* Okay, it was four. Last night, she'd made her decision to walk away. Her life wasn't just the gallery, it needed to be more. And this was one way she could force herself to change. Instead, she smiled. "Dad, I want you to sell the gallery. And you and Mom are going to do just that. I'm looking forward to finding a new path." As the dark cloud lifted from her father's face, she thought that maybe, just maybe, she might even mean the words.

When her father left her office, she dug into the monthly reports. She'd let the paperwork slide for the last week or two. Her boy trouble had left her too busy to do her job. And by God, as long as it was her job, she'd make sure she walked away with a clean conscience. Besides, she would probably need this reference for her next appointment. No need to burn a bridge and hope her contacts in the art world would keep her solvent.

She paused a moment, then went to the website for her favorite airline. Glancing at the calendar and adding two weeks for complications, she booked a flight to Paris without a return ticket. Taylor would figure out the details later, but for now, she had her first stop on her freedom tour. Her parents would be happy for her. Too bad she didn't feel the same way.

Her stomach growled, and she glanced at the clock. She'd been reviewing the ongoing contracts for over two hours. Time for lunch. Today, she was going out. Might as well start feeling like the unemployed bum she would be in less than a month's time. Learn to relax, as Brit would say.

Angie was on the phone when she entered the front of the gallery.

"I've got to go," Angie whispered into the phone. She quickly hung up and stood to greet Taylor. "Thank you for bringing me back."

Taylor felt the tears well in her eyes. Then Angie threw her arms around her, and Taylor was engulfed in a warm hug. One or two of the unwanted tears fell down her cheeks. "I didn't do anything; I just stopped someone else from being a jerk."

Angie brushed off a stray teardrop. "You stood up for me. And I'll never forget that."

Taylor smiled. "I should be thanking you. Mike was off the rails and out of control. If Jesse and your lawyer hadn't told me, I would have thought you'd quit. The guy had become too controlling."

Angie studied her with a look on her face Taylor couldn't decipher. "Love can make you act crazy."

"That's the problem—I never even saw that coming with Mike. Brit told me he had a thing for me for years, but I always thought we were just friends." Taylor swung her tote bag on her shoulder. "Anyway, I'm heading out to grab a long lunch and maybe even a glass of wine before I come back and tackle the rest of those contract reviews. I have my cell if you need me."

"Take your time. We'll be fine. Brit just left to grab a pizza for us, and she's going to teach me how to set up a display." Angie beamed. "She says I have a knack for visual placement."

"You'll be running the place before Jesse knows it." Taylor cringed at the words. She could see the family involved in the gallery. Picking artists and giving their own twist on the art world, just like she and her grandfather had done when she started working with him. Grief stabbed at her heart. For a minute, she wasn't sure if the pain was caused by losing her grandfather, the gallery, or her connection with Jesse and his family.

"He cares about you," Angie said, interrupting her thoughts.

Taylor smiled and shook her head. "I'm afraid I've closed that door. However, I know he cares about you. You told them about the cancer, didn't you?"

"I told Jesse when I got that lawyer letter. Then he brought in the entire group. I swear, that boy can't keep a secret to save his life."

"You'll appreciate the support later. Don't be so stubborn—it's nice to have family." Taylor paused at the door. "But, if you ever need something, you know you can call me too."

Angie nodded, then waved Taylor out the door. "Go to lunch. We can sing 'Kumbaya' and roast marshmallows when you get back."

Taylor left the gallery, and as she walked past the large picture windows she saw Angie pick up the phone.

•••

An hour later, filled with seafood, pasta, garlic bread, and not one, but two glasses of wine, Taylor strolled back to the gallery. She'd stopped in a dress shop and picked up a new purse that she had seen in the window as she passed the storefront. She patted the new bag on her shoulder as she walked. Impulse purchase or not, it represented her new life. The canvas tote was huge with hand-painted purple pansies strung across the outside. She'd been able to stuff her old bag inside with no problem. Time to take care of Taylor. She might even take the rest of the afternoon off and go walk through the art museum.

Taylor swung open the door to the gallery, deciding to do just that. She'd take a cab down to the museum and walk away this pleasant buzz she felt.

"Angie? Brit?" No one was at the front desk. Odd, but Angie had mentioned they were working on a display. She dumped her bag behind the counter and headed toward the first display room. Empty. Frowning, she stepped farther into the gallery. Her stomach clenched and the pleasant buzz in her head disappeared fast. Something felt wrong.

Entering the last display room, she saw the picture. The room had been draped in all black, letting a single light shine on the painting. A painting of her.

Taylor walked up to the easel and studied the lines. The way her smile teased and her eyes in the portrait danced, she almost looked like a Renaissance model. She half expected to find fat cherubs circling her nearly naked form. Instead, the rest of the picture was set in a bed. Sheets tangled, keeping her modest, but hinting at a perfect body that she knew didn't quite match her own.

"Do you like it?"

The question came from behind her. Jesse. She didn't turn when she answered. "You did this? How?"

"From your sitting at your mom's class. Of course, I played with the surroundings a bit." Jesse's voice sounded closer now. She could almost feel his hand on her back, supporting her.

"Typically, it takes several sittings to finish a portrait like this. You did it from just one?" She turned, challenging him. If she'd found out he'd taken pictures of her when she was asleep, she was going to kill him.

"The rest was from memory. Believe me, you're hard to get out of my thoughts." Jesse took her hand. "I need to ask you something."

She wanted to pull away. She felt a jolt of energy run through her body as he held her hand. Something so simple shouldn't feel so sexual. Shouldn't make her want to kiss him. "I don't think we have anything to talk about. I'm getting the office ready for the transition. You should be able to work directly with Brit on any questions you have."

"You didn't read the proposal George drafted." Jesse stepped closer.

Taylor shrugged. "No need. Angie shouldn't have been fired. It was a mistake, and one I've corrected, so you didn't need to convince me to keep her on."

Jesse stared at her hand and the look made her shiver. "I didn't just want Angie to stay on. The papers said you'd stay on as manager after the sale."

Taylor sighed. "We both know that's not going to happen."

"Why not? We make a good team—as long as we're completely honest with each other."

Taylor laughed. "When have we been honest? We always seem to be doing this dance. If I'm chasing, you're running. And if you chase . . . "

"You run. I get it. You need more of a commitment."

"Like a painting of me in your bed." Taylor turned back to the painting. It was hauntingly beautiful, not because she was beautiful, but because the artist had painted her that way.

"I never said it was my bed. But no, that isn't what I'm talking about." Jesse paused. "I know I'm not in your league. But I'm going to take a chance here. If you say no, I'll quit bothering you. You can stay on as manager, or not, it's your choice."

"So you're asking me to keep running the gallery?" Taylor kept her voice steady, even though she wanted to scream, or turn and kiss the heck out of the man next to her. How could he mess with her feelings so much? No one ever got her this worked up. No one, except Jesse.

"No. I mean, yes, but that's not my question." He took her shoulders and spun her around to face him. As she searched his eyes, he kneeled before her.

This can't be happening, she thought. *No way. I'm misunderstanding the action.* As she watched, Jesse pulled a ring out of his shirt pocket.

He held the diamond up to her. "Taylor DeMarco, will you marry me?"

"Have you lost your mind?" Taylor stared at the perfect marquise-cut diamond in a platinum setting. It couldn't have been more perfect if she'd chosen the ring herself. Brit had to have had a hand in this decision. Her mind raced. Marry Jesse. She glanced at the painting.

Jesse sighed, running a hand through his hair. "Probably. I can't sleep, food tastes like sawdust, and all I've been able to focus on for weeks is that painting. So, insanity is an option. Is that a no? I'm feeling a little foolish down here on one knee, especially if you're going to blow me off." Jesse rubbed his thumb over the top of her knuckles. "Think about it. We're good together."

"When we're not trying to kill each other." Taylor's heart was going to beat out of her chest. So this was what it felt like. She felt scared, disoriented, and ecstatic, all at the same time.

"Life will never be dull. We have passion." Jesse squeezed her hand. "I can't imagine going through the rest of my life without you. When we met, something in me awoke, like I'd been asleep for a really long time. And honestly, that scared me. You weren't a one-night stand."

"Two." Taylor reminded him.

"Fine, two-night stand. Stop interrupting me, woman, I'm trying to make a point."

"Yes, sir," Taylor said, stifling a laugh.

"Anyway, you scared the crap out of me. I know love doesn't come to everyone. I'm not stupid enough to throw it away when it does. Someone once told me to marry the person I can't live without. That's you."

"I think it's from a movie. Don't marry the person you can live with, but the one you can't live without." Taylor broke her gaze away from Jesse and looked at the picture. "Do you really see me like that?"

Jesse swore under his breath. "No, I couldn't get the right look. You're so much more beautiful than I could hope to draw."

She turned back, her free hand waving at the portrait. "Oh, Jesse, I could never be this beautiful."

This time he stood and pulled her into his arms. "To me, you are." He then captured her lips in a deep, slow kiss.. A kiss that was more of a promise than a desire. When he stopped, he stared into her eyes, pausing just a moment before asking, "Will you marry me?"

She took the ring away from him. "I just bought a ticket to Paris for next month."

"So that's a no?" Pain flitted across Jesse's face.

Taylor shook her head and slipped the diamond on her left ring finger. "That's a yes, but my ticket better be refundable."

This time when he kissed her, she felt the room moving under them. "I'll eat the cost if it isn't."

Chapter 16

The first weekend in May was unseasonably warm that year. Lizzie and James had pushed off the seasonal opening of Hudson's Spa, the rural bed and breakfast retreat they ran, for a week, letting the family take over the four cabins surrounding their home. James had been busy remodeling the big house to add more bedrooms. The twins were getting kicked out of the nursery to make room for a new arrival coming that fall.

"I swear, you're carrying a girl," Angie said, patting Lizzie's stomach. They sat around a picnic table out in the large backyard, enjoying the spring sunshine next to the riverbank. Angie's hair was spiky, short, and gray—a look she'd sported after being able to give up her scarf collection. She donated all the scarves to a cancer support group for newly diagnosed members. "You're carrying her totally differently than you did the boys."

"That's because there's just one growing in there." Lizzie laughed. "Not that we don't want a girl, I just don't want to jinx it."

"Be careful what you wish for," Barb said. "I never thought raising a girl would be the challenge Kadi's putting us through. Did you know she wants her ears pierced? Apparently she's the only child in her class that can't wear earrings. And don't get me started on the makeup argument." Barb leaned over and touched her newborn son's foot sticking out of the blanket covering the car seat. "Grey won't give us half the trouble Kadi does."

"Don't count on it. Boys are different." Angie sipped on her iced tea. "I'll take her next weekend and get her ears pierced. You should have told me—I would have done it last month when we went clothes shopping."

"Hunter would have a cow if she came home with studs in her ears." Barb dipped a chip into the homemade salsa. "Let's just give him some time to adjust to the pre-teen years, okay?"

"I just don't see the problem. Let the girl live. She's already had a taste of how unfair and short life can be. Losing her folks that young could have made her a basket case instead of turning into a horse nut." Angie ran her hand through her hair. "Take it from someone who knows."

"Believe me, I realize that every day." Barb unhooked Grey from his carrier and sat the boy on her lap, kissing his bald head.

Angie glanced around the gathering, "Angelic was spot on with her prediction."

Lizzie frowned. "What prediction?"

"She said if Jesse bought the gallery, change would happen." Angie waved her hands indicating the yard. "And look at all the changes."

"It's called life, Angie. Life happened, not a fortuneteller's prediction." Barb held her palm flat for Grey to explore with his tiny fingers.

Angie sniffed. "Whatever you want to believe. I just know the woman is a godsend with her counsel."

The women wore sundresses, shorts, and sandals for the parade. They waited for the boys to get ready to go. JR and James had gone ahead with the horse trailer, as they were riding as part of JR's horse club. The twins ran around the edges of the yard playing chase with Kadi, who looked more like the child she was than the teenager she'd soon be. Hunter sat alone near the river, watching the water sparkle over the rocks.

Only two people were missing. Jesse and Taylor.

• • •

"I should wear the suit." Jesse reached for the black suit lying out on the bed. Taylor slapped his hand.

155

"You look great." She smoothed his button-down shirt, flipping his too-long hair over the shirt collar. "A suit is overkill. You wanted to have your first show here as part of Shawnee Rodeo Weekend. Now you have to dress like a cowboy, or all the critics will be disappointed."

"I wanted to get away from the bull rider stigma. What was I thinking?" He sank onto the bed and put his head in his hands.

Taylor sat next to him. "Your show is going to be amazing. I've already heard from six of the major art sites. They have people here from Boise just for today's opening. Bull riding is what you did, not who you are."

"Tell that to Angie. I swear, she was showing everyone who walked into the studio last week photos from the championship last winter." He took her hand. "You really think they'll like the show?"

"You're a talented artist. Why do you think DeMarco Gallery is sponsoring your show?" She kissed his cheek.

"Because I own the gallery?" He smiled. "I hear the tribe getting anxious out there. We better make our appearance."

She stood and put her hand on his chest. "I love you, Jesse Sullivan."

He kissed her, slowly and sweetly]. "I love you, Taylor DeMarco Sullivan."

He went to step away but she held him.

"Seriously, they'll come looking for us in about three minutes. Lizzie won't miss JR riding in the parade." He squeezed her hand. "I don't have time to ravage you on the bed, or in the hot tub."

"In your dreams." Taylor bit her lip. "I just wanted to tell you one thing before we met up with your family. Something you should know. Although, I'm not sure how happy you're going to be."

"Oh God, you've already heard from the critics. They hate the show. They hate me." Jesse searched her face. "Wait, you look happy. They liked me?"

"No. I mean, I don't know." She took a deep breath. "What I need to tell you, before we go meet with your family, is that we have a family right here. In this room."

Jesse laughed. "Oh, honey, I know. You're my family now. It's just, the Sullivans are pretty in-your-face close, especially when we all get together. You'll get used to it."

She held him tight as he tried to step away. "Listen to me. We're a family. You, me, and ..." Taylor let her gaze drop down to her stomach. "Lizzie's not the only one expecting a new arrival."

Jesse's eyes widened. "You're pregnant? What, when?"

"Well, I'm pretty sure it happened on our trip to Sun Valley a few months ago. I thought I was just busy, that I had forgotten. But when I started feeling sick, Brit took me to the doctor last week. We're having a baby."

Jesse picked her up and swung her around the cabin bedroom. "A baby."

As they walked out to the backyard to tell the family about their newest addition, Taylor felt tears fill her eyes. She saw the picture take shape in front of her. Their life had become a painting Norman Rockwell could have done; one called *A Summer Gathering*. Family. Messy, crazy, and most of all, loving. Her family now.

She was a Sullivan.

About the Author

Lynn Cahoon's a multi-published author. An Idaho native, her stories focus around the depth and experience of small town life and love. Lynn is published in the *Chicken Soup* anthologies, has explored controversial stories for the confessional magazines, has short stories in *Women's World*, and contemporary romantic fiction. Currently, she's living in a small historic town on the banks of the Mississippi river where her imagination tends to wander. She lives with her husband and four fur babies. She can be found at her *website*.

More from This Author
(From *The Bull Rider's Manager* by Lynn Cahoon)

If flying was hell, waiting to fly was purgatory. Their plane should have taken off an hour ago. And even though they were on hold, Jesse Sullivan still hadn't graced the airport with his presence. Barb dialed Jesse's cell again and immediately got his answering message. "Damn, Jesse—where are you?"

"No luck?" Hunter Martin, prodigal son of Martin Dairy Empires—and potential sponsor for her perpetually late client—opened his blue eyes and looked at her.

Barb had thought the man had been asleep when she'd pulled out the cell one more time. She pasted on a smile she didn't feel. "Just his voice mail. Maybe he's stuck in traffic?"

Hunter raised his eyebrows. "In Boise?"

"It happens," Barb shot back. "He's been staying at his brother's spread up near Lucky Peak so maybe a logging truck accident slowed him down."

Hunter shook his head. "Really?"

"It could happen. Those trucks fly on those narrow roads." Barb sighed. "I think you're stuck with me for the flight. I don't think Jesse will make it."

"I'm not going to complain." Hunter's smile was slow and sexy. He closed his eyes again. "Shake me if they announce our flight. I didn't get much sleep last night."

Barb smiled. I bet you didn't. Hunter Martin was known in Boise social circles as a player. Or at least he had been. All Barb really knew about the thirty-two-year old bachelor was that he liked the Country Star bar—well known for its line dancing classes and generous beer prices—better than the upscale places downtown. She'd seen him at Country Star a few years ago and man, the boy could swing. In all her years around the rodeo, Barb had never been able to relax enough to let her partner lead her around the dance floor. But she felt the music, even if her dancing would put her on a reality show for the Worst Dancers in America.

Rumor had it that Mr. Martin must be involved because he'd been absent from his usual bar stool for months. Barb snuck a glance at his left hand. No ring yet. Although that didn't mean anything. He still could be engaged.

Barb wished she'd just taken a direct flight to San Francisco. But since she'd had to come up to get another caretaker hired and settled with Mom, she'd jumped at the chance to host a potential new sponsor for the weekend. Martin Dairy had big promotion pockets. Or at least that's what was rumored. And the company loved to sponsor bull riders. Jesse better not screw this up.

Going into partnership with James, Jesse's brother, and becoming Jesse's manager when James had wanted to get off the road to run Hudson's Spa with Lizzie, his new wife, had seemed like a no brainer. James, Lizzie, and Jesse had been friends since high school in Shawnee. And Barb had managed cowboys for years. She'd taken newcomers from small town rodeos and gotten them into the finals in Las Vegas in no time. But Jesse already had a champion belt buckle. And acted like it. The man was infuriating, at best.

Hunter's pocket started to vibrate and Barb jumped back, hoping the man hadn't caught her staring.

Hunter pulled out his Blackberry. Bringing the phone in front of his face before opening his eyes, he squinted at the display. Frowning, he stood. "Sorry, I've got to take this."

Barb watched the man walk away. Cowboy casual in Wranglers and a cotton button-down shirt, Hunter could have been her wayward bull rider. His dark hair had just the right curl, making Barb's finger's itch to play with it. The man would give any of the rodeo guys a run for their money in the body department, even though Barb knew Hunter spent his days in a high rise in Boise, managing the large dairy operation. Martin Dairy didn't just own one dairy farm in the valley. Rumor had it that old man Martin wanted to wipe out the competition and be the only milk producer around. They'd bought out the cheese factory in the next town a few years ago, and now Martin Dairy brand cheese was on supermarket shelves nationwide.

Barb sighed. She could imagine the fun Hunter would be if he weren't a potential sponsor. And if she weren't Jesse's manager. She'd just have to put the drool worthy man out of that part of her mind. Just for the weekend. She shook her head. She needed a life outside the rodeo. A man she could come home to and he'd massage her shoulders. Someone she could tell her dumb stories to who'd laugh and understand. Someone who didn't mind that she traveled every weekend from late April to December. At twenty-six, she felt like the old maid of the group, especially since Lizzie and James tied the knot.

Yeah, like that was going to happen.

Her cell phone buzzed. Without glancing at the display, she answered. "Where are you?"

"In my living room, why, was I supposed to be somewhere else?" Her mother's voice quivered.

Barb leaned back in her chair. "No, Mom. I just thought you were someone else. What's going on?"

Her mother's voice dropped. "There's someone in the house."

"Cassie. Her name's Cassie." Barb watched Hunter pace the walkway, a smile on his lips. Yep, there was a woman in the man's life. She wondered what the mystery girlfriend thought of him taking a weekend alone to go to a rodeo?

"How do you know her name?" Lorraine Carico hissed into the phone. "She just showed up with bags like she was moving in my house."

"Mom, she is moving in. She's a trained nurse's aide and she'll help you with the house. You've been saying you need someone to help around the house." Barb sighed. This wasn't the first time she'd told her mom why Cassie was there. In fact, this wasn't the first live-in nurse's aide that Barb had hired to help her mom. But each time, the transition was getting harder and harder.

"You hired her?" Lorraine's voice sounded hesitant, uncertain.

"I hired her yesterday. Remember, she came to the house and we talked to her? She barrel raced as a teenager. She went to high school in McCall." Barb tried to clue her mother in to the conversation and why Cassie had been such a great match. Why Barb hoped her mother's stories about how she'd dominated the rodeo queen circuit when she was young wouldn't bore the young woman to death.

"Well, if she barrel raced, I bet she'd like to see my trophy room." Her mom's voice sounded stronger.

Barb noticed jean clad legs in front of her. She looked up into the concerned eyes of Hunter. Cocking her head, she covered the phone and asked, "What's going on?"

"They just called our boarding group." Hunter nodded to the gate where people were lining up.

"Mom, I've got to go. The plane is boarding." Barb sighed. She glanced toward the line. Business had to come first, at least today, but she wanted to rent a car and return to her mom's house.

"Plane? Where are you going?" Lorraine's voice turned into a sob. "Why are you leaving?"

"I have to go to work." Barb stood up and grabbed her briefcase with her tablet and the tons of contracts she needed to review for her guys. Barb heard a gentle voice asking her mother to let her talk to Barb.

Cassie's cheerful voice came over the phone. "Sorry, I'll get her calmed down. Have a great flight. Man, I wish I was going to Vegas. I hear it's a great party."

Barb smiled. "I don't seem to have time for the party piece anymore. Thanks, Cassie." She clicked off the phone and followed Hunter to the gate. Countryside Homes had a room on reserve for her mom. Switching caretakers was getting harder and harder. Her mom was taking longer to acclimate. Maybe Barb had made a mistake in trying to stretch out the money with just one more at home caretaker. Maybe it had been time. Exhaustion racked her body. She shouldn't have to be making these decisions, not now. This was supposed to be her time.

"Everything okay?" Hunter asked, concern lacing his voice.

Barb squared her shoulders. "You know family. And since I'm an only child, there's no one to share the wealth with ... " For the second time in less than thirty minutes, Barb pasted on her made-for-television smile. "No worries. Now, do you want the window or aisle seat?"

Hunter watched her for a few minutes then answered, "Whatever you don't want. I'm easy."

Barb hoped that was true. If Martin Dairy came on board as Jesse's sponsor and Jesse pulled it together enough to win the championship again this year, she could afford to put her mom in Countryside. Then maybe Barb wouldn't worry so much about her.

And maybe pigs would fly. She glanced around the boarding aircraft for a pink pig, waiting to take her flight to Nevada, and giggled.

• • •

Hunter snuck a peek at the woman sitting next to him on the plane. He couldn't believe how beautiful she was. Flame red hair, porcelain skin, and a killer body. When she smiled at him, man, his heart melted. Or would have if he had a heart, he reminded himself. Kati owned that piece of real estate—or at least she did until she went away to college. But that was years away.

In an odd way, Barb reminded him of his spit-fire niece. Kati and the older woman looked nothing alike, but both had that twinkle in their eyes. The one that showed up just as he realized he was being played.

No, he was glad the bull rider had missed this flight. Very glad.

He leaned back in his seat and waited for the plane to take off. Even though he flew regularly now that he had taken over the marketing division for Martin Dairy, he still hated take offs. And landings. The piece in the middle was just fine, especially when the flight attendant started serving drinks.

The way Barb gripped the seat arms, he figured she wouldn't say no to a beer. Or two. "You might want to relax that grip, slugger, at least until the pilot starts to taxi to the runway."

He watched her look at him in confusion and when he looked down at her hands, her gaze followed his. She released her hands, stretching out her fingers. "I didn't even notice. You'd think I'd get use to this. But it never happens. I guess I'm just too type A to allow someone else to fly the plane."

"Don't tell me the Renaissance woman is a pilot as well."

Barb chuckled. "No, just a control freak."

"As soon as they get us up, I'll order a few beers. We'll have to drink fast though, Las Vegas isn't that far."

"Believe me, I can chug with the best of them. Occupational hazard when you manage bull riders." Barb turned away from the window and faced Hunter.

"I'm curious. Whatever made you decide to get into this business? Seems more suited for … " Hunter paused, searching for a word.

"Suited for a man? Or were you going to say a retired bull rider?" Barb set her shoulders, waiting for his answer. "Because if you go all nineteen-fifties on me, I'm going to have to deck you.

Mom at home raising kids, dad going to work, you know that's a dream life, right?"

"I was going to say someone more stodgy. You know, like those big belly businessmen that hang around the corrals, trying to land the next Lane Frost or Tuff Hedeman. All dressed up in what they think passes as rodeo gear, or maybe did twenty years ago." Hunter smiled. "Believe me, if you had come to talk to me about my future when I was riding, college would have been out the window."

Barb tilted her head. "I didn't know you rode. Your file doesn't mention it."

Hunter laughed. "You mean the press release version of Hunter Martin, the youngest marketing director in Martin Dairy history? I would have thought a smart girl like you would see through the public relations crap."

"Other than the file your company has been distributing, there isn't much else out there on you. I know where you like to drink your tequila shots but that's from hanging out in the same dives when I'm home. I know you were voted most likely to succeed and most likely to make a movie by thirty by your senior class." Barb smiled seductively. "Was that because of your drama credits or your smile?"

"Mostly because of my reputation as a high school Casanova. There were just too many pretty girls and not enough days in the week. I had to learn to juggle."

"Juggle women?" Now both of Barb's eyebrows rose.

"Dates. And mix in football games and debate. Believe me, it's a losing concoction. I had a party at my house one night when the folks were out of town and seven girls who thought we were dating showed. After that fiasco, I kept it down to one girl at a time." Hunter grinned.

"Very sporting of you." Barb shook her head. "Too bad Jesse's not here. I'm sure he could match you story for story. At least in the dating department. That boy was trouble the day he landed on this earth."

"You've known him a long time?" Hunter felt a stab of jealousy. Maybe there was more to Barb and Jesse than just manager and client.

"Jesse was a year younger at Shawnee. I guess I've known him forever. I don't really remember him until Lizzie, she's my best friend, started dating James freshman year. Everywhere James went his little brother followed. He was a funny kid, I mean funny, ha ha, not funny weird."

"So you guys grew up in the same town?" This was sounding worse and worse. The two had history together.

"Shawnee, Idaho. Population five hundred and one as of today. But Lizzie's expecting twins so that will bump up the census soon." Barb smiled. "Shawnee's famous in local circles for the earliest rodeo of the season. First weekend of May, sun, rain, or snow."

"I think I went up for a rodeo with my frat brothers when I was in college. Pretty much a weekend party more than just a rodeo."

Barb laughed. "That's Shawnee. Hell, the whole town gets involved. The churches have yard sales, the school has a quilt show, and the FFA sells water and hot dogs for the parade."

"All I remember are the bars. Man, those rodeo chicks can dance."

"And now you're on your way to Vegas. I'm sure you can find a gal or two who will two-step with you," Barb teased.

"This trip isn't about the party. I told Dad I'll let you do your dog and pony show before I made up my mind about the sponsorship. And the rodeo is part of that show, although I think you're missing your dog."

Barb frowned. "Jesse will be there."

When she didn't elaborate, Hunter glanced down the aisle for the flight attendant. They'd talked all the way through the takeoff and the keeper of the beer was two aisles away. "So now that I've stuck my foot in my mouth, do you want a beer?"

Hunter could see Barb fighting a grin. "That would be lovely."

"Maybe dinner when we land?" Hunter gave the order to the flight attendant.

"This is a working trip for me, you know." Barb glanced out the window at the still bright sky.

"Your star bull rider isn't even in town tonight. And isn't convincing me to sponsor him your real job this trip?" Hunter knew he was playing the sponsor card, pushing for time with her, but, man, he wanted to keep that smile on her face directed at him.

"That's the trouble with you sponsors. You all think it's all about you."

"I don't think that."

Barb took the beer the flight attendant offered. "You don't?"

Hunter popped open the can, took a swig, then answered. "Of course not. It's all about the money."

Also look for Lynn Cahoon's *The Bull Rider's Brother*
In the mood for more Crimson Romance?
Check out *Paradise Point* by Dana Volney
at *CrimsonRomance.com*.